Gichigami

Gichigami

a novel

LINDSEY STEFFES

UNIVERSITY OF MASSACHUSETTS PRESS
Amherst and Boston

ISBN 978-1-62534-850-0 (paper)

Designed by Sally Nichols
Set in Minion Pro
Printed and bound by Books International, Inc.

Cover design by adam b. bohannon
Cover photo by Athony: *Lake Superior sunset and moon on the
north shore in Minnesota*. Adobestock.com 467480668.

Library of Congress Cataloging-in-Publication Data

Names: Steffes, Lindsey, 1991- author.
Title: Gichigami / Lindsey Steffes.
Description: Amherst : University of Massachusetts Press, 2025. | Series: Juniper
prize for fiction
Identifiers: LCCN 2024032690 (print) | LCCN 2024032691 (ebook) | ISBN
9781625348500 (paperback) | ISBN 9781685751241 (ebook) | ISBN 9781685751258
(epub)
Subjects: LCGFT: Bildungsromans. | Novels.
Classification: LCC PS3619.T44753 G53 2025 (print) | LCC PS3619.T44753 (ebook)
| DDC 813/.6--dc23/eng/20240715
LC record available at https://lccn.loc.gov/2024032690
LC ebook record available at https://lccn.loc.gov/2024032691

British Library Cataloguing-in-Publication Data
A catalog record for this book is available from the British Library.

Mooniingwanekaaning-minis (Madeline Island). National Park Service.
Accessed March 1, 2024. https://www.nps.gov/media/video/view.htm
?id=E141BFE3-09DD-4DBE-99F0-F9CB1B6DC4E0.
No protection is claimed in original U.S. Government works.

Steffes, Lindsey. "Gichigami." *Midwestern Gothic*: Issue 17, February 2015.

For my father
For Susie & Benny

Gichigami

Madeline Island, Wisconsin
1998

CHAPTER ONE

Marta

There was a dip in the island, and right between two ancient firs my house grew like a weed. Dad was a carpenter— like Jesus, he'd often say. "Not as crafty with a handsaw but far more practiced with a power tool." This winter, like most, he'd been laid off for the whole season. He kept busy making add-ons to the house: another level to the attic, a ten-foot lookout stacked on top of that, crowned with a rusty, shrieking weathervane.

One December morning, I tiptoed out onto the porch and stood there barefoot, hopping from one leg to the other, watching Dad rework the chimney high on the roof.

"Easy on the left side," I hollered. "I think it's going to tip."

So Dad threw a few more bricks onto the right side to balance things out. And he kept going like that, adding bricks and mortar and still more bricks, until the chimney reached right up to the sky, until the smoke became the clouds because you couldn't tell where one started and the other stopped. Come springtime, our house would be a castle. We'd tower above the whole island, taller than the lighthouse, taller than the geese could fly. They'd have to get a ladder just to ring our bell, a pulley for the mailman.

Dad wiped his forehead, staring proudly at the never-ending chimney, at the scale of our house. He leaned against the lookout, running his hand along the siding, flaking off large slivers of white paint. "Marta," he called down, frowning at the pieces in his hand. "We've got to repaint before it snows again. Pick a color, whatever you want."

"Blue," I hollered, shaking the birds from the trees. "Blue as the ocean."

"Never seen the ocean."

"Check a postcard." No time to explain.

Bare feet stinging with cold, I hopped back inside, threw on my pom-pom stocking cap, a thick pair of wool socks, and Dad's rubber boots. I wound duct tape around the soles to keep out the snow and tucked lamb's wool around my ankles. I opened the closet and rifled through jackets. I knew what I was looking for: two black marble eyes staring up from the collar. I found Mom's mink coat, wrapped it around me, and walked back into the winter light.

"Not that one," Dad said, eyes on the fur.

"What difference does it make?"

He rubbed his jaw. Though he was burly and rough and could fit both of my wrists in one hand, he was never any good at discipline. He was more reactive, angry in a moment, like torrential rain.

"Besides," I said, "I look good. Really good." I spun around, imagining a slow dance with Levi, one of the Red Cliff boys who grew up dancing.

Dad shrugged. "Whatever you say." He started packing up his tools, slipping them one by one into his utility belt. Just as I turned to leave, he shouted, "Be careful on the road," something he always said because the road was long and it was made of ice. In the summertime, we took the ferry from our island to the mainland, but in the winter most of Lake Superior froze over, and then we had a road lined with evergreens. Tourists would come all the way up here just to take pictures of it, just to step a few paces onto the ice to say they'd done it, though they always turned back quickly.

"The road," Dad repeated.

"I'll be fine."

I cut through the backyard on a footpath I'd made between massive pines and their massive, armlike branches. There was one particular tree that I "shook hands with" every time I passed. I knew this was stupid, but it was something I did in private. In my mind, it guaranteed safe passage.

After the forest, there was the shoreline, the island's south coast—bright, open, and empty of life, more lonesome in the winter than any place I'd ever been. Standing at the edge of the island and looking out across the lake, I knew the mainland was there on the other side, all the world with it, not so far away. Only two miles. Some days, those miles passed as quickly as a single song on my Walkman and, at other times, they felt longer than a lifetime, so long you swore you'd never make it until you found yourself standing on the other shore, proven wrong. To the tourists, this was the draw of the island. It was the perfect getaway: no traffic, few people. Just a bar, a history museum, a bunch of pretty leaning pines and cabins sagging under the weight of snow.

During high season, we'd always get a few tourists coming up to the house. If the island hadn't needed their money, Dad would've scared them away with a single look, frigid, impassive, from the porch. He wouldn't have even needed his rifle.

"What a wonder to live here" the conversation would go between some old couple in nautical clothes.

"It's like something from the storybooks," the wives would say. "Look at the chimney! Oh, and the wishing well!"

"What kind of wood is that?" the husbands would chime in, pointing at the porch. "Looks like red cedar. Yes," they'd say, leaning closer, "it has to be."

But Dad would shake his head no, telling them about the shipwrecks instead, always a crowd pleaser. With great, jerking hand motions, he'd tell them how he had scuba-dived in Lake Superior, which was, of course, the deepest and darkest of all the Great Lakes. And how he'd harvested the wood himself from the *Smith Moore*, a wooden steam barge sunk in 1889, now under ninety feet of water. Ninety. And how the wives would gasp! And how the husbands would still swear it was red cedar!

I crossed the icy sand, passing over long-abandoned beach toys: a deflated hot dog—or was it a banana?—that tourists had ridden last summer, a paddleboat carcass, a pair of kayaks left tied to the dock and frozen in place.

Only a few steps onto the ice road, I could feel the cold setting in, the wind picking up. Out on the lake, the snow was blowing crosswise so that everything was white and endless and all mixed together. The snow, the ice, the sky. You couldn't tell up from down. I tracked the painted edge of the road so I wouldn't get lost.

Last winter, a couple of kids on vacation from the Cities had sneaked out of their parents' hotel and tried crossing over to the island, but lost the road. The year before, it had happened to a group of Rover Scouts, some well-equipped backpackers all the way from Sweden. Their motto, "Be prepared! Always prepared!," headlined the local paper, except with a question mark. And years before, it had happened to a local woman who should've known better. "Her husband left her," my mom's friend Sylvia had said, dragging one index finger across her neck.

None of the missing were recovered.

Dad said they must've fallen through the ice. A lake that size was more like an ocean. Too deep to freeze everywhere. Their bodies were lost, but someday they'd be discovered: skin like porcelain, hair drifting around them, fingernails white and long. Preserved at the bottom of the lake. There had been over five hundred shipwrecks. Some 10,000 bodies claimed by the lake. I wanted to swim down as far as I could and touch their frozen limbs. Grab hands and feet and hair and drag them up to shore. Under the hot sun, maybe they'd come alive again. Maybe they'd love me for having found them.

By the time I reached the mainland, my hands were so numb they felt like they didn't belong to me anymore. The winter was deep within my chest, and I wondered how long it'd take for my body to freeze inside and out like the deer carcasses Dad kept strung up in the garage.

I walked along the shore until I reached Onie's. I stood on the porch for a second, fished in my pocket for a comb beneath the mothballs, and ran it through a couple of times. Trying to look presentable.

"Hell-oooo," I said, knocking. "Ms. Bonnie. You home?"

I could hear footsteps on the stairs. The door cracked open, one eye peering out. Dark brown, light at the edges.

"None of you kids call ahead. I'm busy, little miss. Come back tomorrow."

"You've got eyes like two sunflowers. The prettiest in town." I smiled, pressing my weight against the door.

"Enough, Marty." She swung the door out. "Hurry up. The cold."

As I followed Onie up the stairs, her bones creaked louder than the boards beneath her. She was seventy-nine years old, a Red Cliff Band of Lake Superior Chippewa elder who hated tourists and people without manners and me, when I was bugging her. She taught me about the history of this place. Gichigami ("great sea," a great lake or body of water) is the Ojibwe word for Lake Superior. The Ojibwe have been here for hundreds of years. They had built a settlement on the island. Navigated the archipelago in birchbark canoes. Harvested wild rice, fished year round, told great stories. The French descended upon them in the 1600s—explorers, fur trappers and traders, and Jesuit priests, all of whom tried to make their home on the island, which was not just any old island. Madeline Island, Mooniingwanekaaning ("island of the yellow shafted flicker"), was special to the Ojibwe—their spiritual center, which Onie reminded me every time I complained about living all the way out there.

When we reached the top of the stairs, Onie led me into her sewing room, crowded with heaps and heaps of fabric. There were dresses in every color hung up along the curtain rods like window shades, half-finished beadwork piled high on her desk, and powwow regalia packed inside her closet, jingles and feathers and fringe spilling out. Onie wouldn't go to the summer powwows. She said they were overrun with tourists. But she loved making the regalia, sitting on the bleachers on a cool summer night and watching the dancers practice.

"Who you wearing a dress for?" Onie nodded to a wedding photo of her and her first husband, married at the chapel at the top of the hill. It struck me, how big they were smiling, how everyone seemed happy at first.

"Nothing white." I could feel myself blushing. "Make it blue. Lots of sequins."

She stooped down and started picking through stacks of fabric, pulling out pinks.

"Blue," I repeated as if she'd already forgotten. She was old, after all. "You want me to write that down?"

"I could do it in my sleep." She nodded toward the door. "I'm busy, remember? Come back tomorrow."

"How much is it gonna be?" There was a rumpled dollar in my pocket, some change. She knew I didn't have enough.

"Don't worry. We'll work something out."

That meant chores: carting her donate items to so-and-so's garage sale, mowing the lawn. She winked at me, shooed me down the stairs.

The cold felt good on the way out. I made my way from the beach, past the row of bungalows, and up the hill to town, which was nothing more than a strip of stores: a couple of souvenir shops closed for winter; Mimi's Moonlight Serenade, a place full of mannequins in underwear; Lucy's grocery store, four aisles wide; and three different bars—the Office, Gem, and the Midnight Girls, each in flickering neon. Once, I saw a Midnight Girl stumble lazily out of the bar and lean up against the pink-lit windows. She smoked a cigarette and plucked holes in her fishnets. "What do you want, little sister?" she called to me, smirking. "Your daddy in here?"

I hurried past her on the sidewalk.

"Bet I know him."

I turned back and looked at her. She wasn't smirking anymore. Her mouth was pinched around the cigarette. She sucked in and flicked the ash at me. "Tall. Quiet. Doesn't drink," she said. "Handsome. Had to be, right? To make a pretty girl like you."

I blushed, and she let out this awful laugh. "Bet he's at the bar right now. Drinking O'Doul's. Spinning that AA chip."

Halfway down the street, I could still hear her laughing. Did she really know Dad? Had he touched her? No, he never went out. He was at home, browning beef, probably wondering where the heck I was.

Today when I passed the Midnight Girls, I kept my eyes up. At the very top of the hill, the chapel stood alone, its sharp, rotting steeple marking the end of town. I'd rarely been past it. And I'd never been inside the chapel itself. It had been closed for thirteen years, a few months before I was born. Apparently, the priest couldn't stand long winters. With the parish funds, he'd flown south. Dad said Mom tried to baptize me herself, dipping my head into the freezing lake as I screamed and screamed. That was easier, she'd said, than driving to the next town over. And what was the difference anyhow? Water was water. God was *everywhere*.

Jaybird's Diner was at the end of the strip. I pushed in, escaping the cold, and went to the counter. Without asking, Sylvia handed me a Coke, a bunch of maraschino cherries floating at the top. I sat there, sipping pop and watching her drop gulps of batter on the grill. The pancakes sprouted up like daisies, full and golden, a reminder of springtime, still five months away.

"Want some?" she asked, a pencil stuck behind her ear.

"Just here to talk."

"About?" She drew the pencil from her ear like she was going to write it down.

"Getting ready for the dance."

"Oh, Marty." She dropped the pencil. "Why bother? Your daddy won't let you go."

"What does he know?"

"More than most men. You'd be surprised."

I knew she only said that because she was after him, along with all the other women on the mainland—all gossips, all trying to get in my ear. Your dad's a real catch, they'd tell me. A prize. A house on the island. A full head of hair.

They thought of him as the same guy from high school, letterman jacket, easy smile. They didn't know he could go a whole day without speaking. Three days if he were really mad.

Sylvia sat down at the counter next to me. "You should listen to your daddy," she said.

"He'll come around."

Sylvia tossed her hair behind her shoulders. In the whole town, she was the only one with red hair. It looked like a bonfire, especially when she heaped it on top of her head. Her lips were red, too. So much fire-red for a woman who looked like she never got enough sleep. Slow blinking eyes, the lazy way she talked, like each word was a dirty dish she had to clear from a table.

"I thought you hated dances," she said.

"Last year was different. I'm older now."

She laughed. "A lot has changed since eighth grade, huh?"

"Oh, I know." She smirked like a devil. "You got a guy, don't you?" There was nothing more annoying than letting her see me blush. "Who's the lucky man?"

"Can't say." Everyone knew she was a blab.

"I bet I know the kid. Spill."

I bit my straw. "I'm getting a dress from Onie. She's making it from scratch."

"Don't change the subject." Sylvia flipped open the notepad

she used for orders and drew a hangman. "Come on, Marty. One game. Let me guess. I promise not to tell your dad."

"You said that last time."

Nothing she could say to that. She sat there pouting. Drawing herself as the hangman.

"You think you could help me with my hair?" I knew this would make her happy.

"Well, duh." She smiled. "Who else?"

"What about your shoes?" she asked. "You gonna wear heels?"

"Don't have any."

"You gonna wear makeup? You should probably wear makeup."

The bell above the door rang. Sylvia jumped up from the counter.

"Customers," she said. "You better go anyway. You got work to do. And Marty—"

"Yeah?"

Her eyes lingered on me. "Nice coat."

At Lucy's, there was only one section with makeup, and it was way in the back because no one ever went there. I sifted through a box of lipstick, making streaks of Nothing but Nude, Ravishing Red, Very Cherry, and Punk Purple along my arm. I was too pale. Nothing looked right.

Just then, Marianne and Chelsea walked in with fresh twenties. They were in the candy aisle, whacking each other with licorice ropes. They looked like identical twins, ice blonde with matching chokers. Abercrombie jeans more expensive than anything I'd ever owned. They had desktop computers and cars they could not yet drive. They talked to senior boys, which was crazy—wasn't it?—freshman year.

Not only were they prettier than most girls in town, they were nice. That was the worst part. If they saw me, the freak in overalls, they might drag me along to one of their sleepover parties or offer me their famous Baby Spice makeover: high, flat-ironed pigtails, pink glossy lips, blue eyeshadow like a pair of black eyes. I'd seen plenty to know.

I hid behind the aisle until they paid and left, and then I left, too, with Black Cherry and Toast of New York, whatever that meant. It wasn't stealing if you tried them on and took them back only a little used, like a library book.

When I got back to the castle, it was sundown. Dad was gone from the roof, but there was a lady standing by our door. Probably a tourist. She wore orange nylons and a pink ruffled peacoat, looking just like a flamingo with her legs stuck two feet deep in the snow.

"Hello?" I said. "You need something?"

The lady didn't turn around. She kept staring up at the castle like she wanted to buy it. It's not for sale, I wanted to tell her, something I'd said to tourists a thousand times.

She ran her fingers against the front door without knocking. I walked closer.

"What are you doing here?" I asked.

The lady stood still. I watched her bright yellow hair move in the wind. After a few seconds, she tilted her chin and looked back at me.

Mom.

CHAPTER TWO

Marta

The last time I saw my mother, she was packing her bags. I was sitting on her bed, watching her iron each of her dresses, drape them over hangers, and tuck them into a worn floral suitcase. "Will you be gone a long time?" I asked.

"I don't know why I bother ironing. The second I pack them up, they're wrinkled all over again."

"Then why don't you stop?"

She put the iron down. I thought she was listening, but then she started up again.

"My mother always ironed everything, and she tore me apart if my clothes weren't pressed," she said. "I hated it, but now I'm the same as her. You will, too, someday."

"Iron everything? I'll never do that."

"No, you'll be just like me."

"I don't want to be like you."

She pressed her lips together tightly. "Oh, min kära, that's just how it works."

A few hours later, she was gone. Dad was tiling the kitchen backsplash like nothing had happened. He never said a word about it, no matter how many times I asked. Occasionally, when we were fighting, when I was feeling especially mean, I'd say, "You're the reason she left." And he'd look at me like I'd driven an auger straight through his heart.

"You really think that," he'd say. Not really a question.

Of course, I did.

He was angry and quiet and impossible to live with. He must have said something. Done something. Bad enough to make her pack her bags and walk down the driveway, away from us, forever. I had watched her disappear, thinking, *Fine, keep walking. Don't look back. We won't miss you. We won't even notice you're gone.* And then she was gone. I couldn't see her from the window. Just the driveway and the snowcapped trees and our empty yard. I sat there for ten minutes, another three hours, waiting for her to turn around. Snow fell and the sun dipped below the trees. When I didn't come for supper, Dad dragged TV trays to the couch and sat with me in front of the window. We ate mac and cheese and ring bologna and stared at our reflections in the dark. Sad empty faces, neither of us hopeful, neither waiting. He had done it this time. She wasn't coming back.

Now she was standing here, a tropical bird caught in the snow, a stupid smile across her face. She shrugged, and her glossy pink purse slipped down her arm. She nudged her floral suitcase with the toe of her high heel as if to say, "Well, I'm back."

I took a sharp breath. "You look old."

Mom looked down at the snow, trying to unbury her feet.

"You look different," I said. "Those stockings. Your hair."

She looked past me, into the window, and tried to smooth the fly-aways in her hair.

"Dad's been adding to the house. It's much bigger since you left. Prettier, too."

Together, we looked up at the castle. My house, not hers.

"You going to say something?" I asked. "You going to tell me where you've been?"

"Aren't you happy to see me?" Her voice was soft and sweet. "You thought I was a stranger."

"You are a stranger."

Mom smiled. She leaned over and tucked my hair behind my ear, dragging her nails slowly against my scalp. It felt wrong, her touching me. Like a character climbing out of the TV.

"Nice coat," she said, running her hand along the fur collar. "Looks familiar."

"Does Dad know you're here?"

"It's a surprise."

"Some surprise."

When she walked into the house, it was like she'd never left. She hooked her purse around the coatrack, went straight to the kitchen, and pulled the teakettle from the cabinet where it had always been.

"You want some?" she asked. "You like tea?"

"That's the sort of thing you should know."

When the tea was ready, we sat across from each other at the oak table Dad had just built from the biggest tree in the woods. She didn't say much, just talked about the snow, the weather, the things strangers said when they were stuck riding the ferry together, cramped on the same bench.

After tea, she wandered through the castle touching things: the carved banister, brand new, the maritime maps tacked on the walls, Dad's row of rubber boots. She stopped at each place, running her fingers along the edges and looking real close like she was checking for dust. I followed her through, watching. She looked so much older now. It showed in her face, in the way she walked, as if the time apart had been longer for her, harder on her body. She was fuller in the middle, skin weathered from years and sun, fine wrinkles blooming from the corners of her mouth. Her smile was severe, her eyes nervous and dark. Almost pretty but no longer beautiful. I had spent so many hours in class imagining Mom at her vanity, slender and poised, dabbing on her prized Dior Diorissimo, lining her lips in something like Toast of New York, asking me, "Well?" when she was finished, smiling, knowing the answer. She was perfect.

Not anymore.

We climbed the stairs to the second floor, Mom straightening frames, step by step. Before I could stop her, she rushed into my bedroom, touching everything: my pillows, my coarse yellow sheets, the clothes on the floor, the clothes spilling from my dresser, Dad's open pocketknife on my nightstand. I wanted to make her leave. But if she walked out, she might never come back. I stood in the doorway, hoping she'd notice the paper snowflakes I had hung in the window with fishing line, a makeshift curtain. After refolding my sheets and straightening the pillowcases, she paused to look through the window. Her hand moved slowly, gently, parting the snowflakes. She peered through the glass into the backyard, sighed deeply, and then slipped past me into Dad's room.

"Looks just the same," she said, thumbing the nick in the dresser.

"We've done a lot since you left."

"The knob on my vanity's still broken. It's just the same."

"Everything's different. We've got a third floor, new rooms, new furniture. Dad says it's Victorian like in the movies."

She smiled. "It feels the same. Just say so."

"It's not the same." I was mad now. "Dad works every day."

"The painting needs work."

"He's going to repaint it. Blue as the ocean. He's probably buying paint right now."

"Why on earth would you paint a house blue?" She was smiling that stupid smile. "Blue of all colors, in December of all months. It's too cold—doesn't he know that? The paint's going to blister."

"We don't care what you think."

She sat on Dad's bed and peeled off her coat. Underneath, she had this gaudy yellow dress on, lightweight, maybe linen. Dressed for another climate. Another planet. She was here finally, and I hated her more than ever.

"I got you something." She reached into her coat pocket and pulled out a box wrapped in white tissue paper.

"What is it?"

"Just open it," she said, so I did, tearing at the corners, making sure to rip the tissue into tiny pieces. Inside the box, a flower.

"It's an orange blossom, min kära, all the way from Florida," she said eagerly, "from my very own backyard."

I cupped the flower in my hand and traced the small white petals, feeling the wax between my fingertips. It smelled sweet like summertime.

Mom leaned closer to me. "Isn't it beautiful? I have an orange tree. Fresh fruit every morning."

"We've got a fruit tree in our backyard. Cherries all summer."

"But those die in the wintertime. In Florida, blossoms come year round. You'd love it."

"I'm never leaving the island," I said, though she wasn't asking. "I don't like warm weather."

"That's not true." Mom pointed to a framed picture on Dad's dresser. "That's you as a baby. Our first vacation. Your father and I borrowed a truck and drove you all the way to Tennessee to see your nana. You cried the whole way there, but the second we stepped out of the truck, you stopped crying. It was the heat. It was the sunlight. I know it."

"It wasn't the heat."

"The sunlight, you loved it."

"I didn't love it."

"Is that any way to speak to your mother?"

"I wouldn't know."

"I haven't been gone that long."

"Since my sixth birthday."

"And you'll be thirteen in March—of course, I remember." Mom reached over, as if to run her fingers through my hair, but stopped short. "But you know something? It feels like yesterday, don't you think?"

"No."

"That long hair, always wild, tangled. The same as when I left you."

"I look different."

"You don't."

Mom lay down flat on the bed, palms up. She closed her eyes. "Look under the bed."

"Go on," she added, knowing I hadn't moved an inch.

I knelt on the floor, reached beneath the bed skirt, and pulled out a paper hatbox. The lid was tight; I had to shimmy it open. I wasn't sure what I was seeing at first. A whole lot of blue. I grabbed what look like shoulders and lifted it out of the box.

A dress. Baby-blue silk chiffon, off-the-shoulder with a big ruffle and a long skirt.

"How did you—?"

"Mothers know," she told me without opening her eyes. "They always know."

I couldn't believe it. Her coming back and her knowing.

"So you can go to the dance," she said.

I hugged the dress to my chest. It was too long. It reeked of cigarettes, a hint of lilac. But it was beautiful, perfect.

"It's a little eighties." She laughed like she would never wear it now. "But you're going to be beautiful. More so than when I wore it."

"Yeah, right."

"You wait. Everyone's going to love you. They'll simply *fall in love.*"

"Everyone?" I pictured a slow dance with Levi, his hands around my waist.

"Everyone."

I wanted to curl myself beside her just for a moment and lay my head against her chest. I could smell hairspray on her curls, that familiar lilac perfume. I wanted to move closer, closer, but she didn't deserve it.

"Dad doesn't want me to go to the dance."

I climbed onto the bed, far enough away so she couldn't touch me. I lay so still, listening to the gentle sound of her breath, the quiet patter of snow upon the roof.

Mom turned on her side to face me and tucked one hand

under her wave of yellow hair. "You're going to be beautiful," she said.

"Dad said no."

"Hush, we'll sleep now. We'll talk about the dance when your father gets back."

It was late, and Dad was still gone. He would be angry she was here with me, in their old room. I couldn't just lie here. I couldn't fall asleep.

"I promise," she whispered. "They'll love you."

She reached out and pressed her hand over mine. I knew it was wrong, her being here, the weight of her hand over mine. But I was so tired. More tired than I realized. And for the first time in a long time, I felt my anger melting.

When Dad finally came home, it was dark. I was sleeping on his bed, still holding the orange blossom.

"Did you see Mom?" I asked, looking around the room, empty now. "She was just here."

"Go to bed," he said roughly. "Your own bed."

"She was here." I squeezed the flower, waiting for Dad to answer, waiting for Mom to reappear from behind the closed bedroom door. Dad yanked it open, but there was nothing but the empty hall.

"Now," he said.

"Where's the dress?" I slipped off his bed and pulled back the covers. I looked under the bed, in the closets, vanity, dresser.

"You took it. She was here," I said.

He grabbed my wrist and yanked me into the hall. I could already feel the bruise forming. "I saw her."

"You didn't."

"You're lying."

"You were fast asleep. Must've had one hell of a dream."

I forced the orange blossom into Dad's hand.

"Where'd you get this?" he said.

"She gave it to me."

"You must've found it at the floral shop."

"It's been closed for two years."

"Then you found it outside, I don't know." He tossed the flower. Its thin white petals flapped and fluttered like the wings of an injured moth, quickly, quickly. It hit the floor.

I scooped it up and ran down the stairs into the kitchen. The teakettle was dry, back in the cabinet. I searched the whole house, every closet. Her floral suitcase was gone. The blue dress gone, too. No heady perfume in the air. No high heels at the door or footprints in the snow. As if Dad were right—she'd never been here.

CHAPTER THREE

Sylvia

Sylvia pinched the fat on her waist, her thighs, and her belly. She turned to the side and stared into her full-length mirror, trying to conjure another body, another person. Anyone.

Her good dress was lying on the floor, the back seam ripped along the zipper. She glared at the pie tin on her nightstand. The diner had done this to her. Forced her to eat and eat—leftovers and feelings and her squashed dreams. They tasted like butter, *heaven*.

She was thirty-four, "feels like" forty-two, with fox-red hair and prominent laugh lines that seemed to mock the sadness of her situation. She was stuck in the middle of nowhere with a collection of Jane Austen paperbacks and a dated one-bedroom apartment. "Retro," she called it, on the rare days when someone visited. Orange shag, velour drapes, a mirrored closet full of JCPenney dresses, tapered jeans, and aprons, all stained from the diner. A television set in the dining room, another in her bedroom, in front of a queen-sized bed, the mattress untouched on one side, on the other a deepening indentation. Cat-themed memorabilia (inherited after her mom stopped chemo). Picture frames filled with people who'd died or left. Oh, how her failed dreams hung around her like stale perfume.

Still, with the right lip liner, with her wild curly hair falling just so, she was beautiful. She was surprised to find her body, which had always seemed unruly to her, impossible to manage, was appealing to men. One customer had called her "Julia Roberts," another "Molly Ringwald." They came in just to see her. No one cared about her size as much as she did.

After she'd failed statistics, chemistry, and home ec and

decided to drop high school, Sylvia had considered moon-lighting as a dancer at the Midnight Girls. It was a small bar down the street with red velvet chairs, a tiny catwalk, and thousands of women's panties hanging from the ceiling. When the Midnight Girls first opened in 1977, Sylvia was thirteen, and she would walk past the bar as often as possible, admiring the neon heart in the window. Sometimes, the women stood outside the door in fur-trimmed suede coats, barefoot or in heels. They wore their hair, usually gold from bleach, parted down the middle, and kept their fingernails in long red ovals. Sylvia did the same. She still did. When she'd mentioned work-ing there, her parents had laughed.

"Have you seen those girls?" her father said. "Athletes."

"Could be models," her mother said.

Later that day, Sylvia applied to be a waitress.

Eighteen years later, she was still waitressing. She kicked her good dress under her bed, pulled on a pair of stirrup leggings and a ratty Wisconsin Badgers sweatshirt with thumbholes at each sleeve. It didn't matter what she wore; Bo wouldn't notice. After years of staring at her across the counter, he had forgotten she was even there. She thought about calling him, breaking something, pouring Dawn into the dishwasher, flooding the kitchen. Then he might come over, help her out.

Sylvia sank into her stiff modular couch, reveling in her own discomfort. No, she wouldn't call Bo. He wouldn't come. Who else?

In a town like this, there was very little to choose from: miners, sailors, bartenders, other women's boyfriends, their husbands. She grabbed her phone, shaped like a sleeping cat, and called Lars. He was ten years younger than Sylvia. He worked in the iron mines and smiled too much for a person who had never left.

Twenty minutes later, he was at her apartment with brandy, bitters, and sugar, an orange to make twists from the rind, and a jar of cherries. "Old fashioneds for an old-fashioned lady," he said, grinning. Every time, the same drinks, the same joke on account of her age. Sylvia plucked out the rinds, gulped down the brandy, and ate the cherries when she was finished, shivering at the sweetness. They made love on the couch. Sylvia left her sweatshirt on.

When he left, minutes later, she straightened the kitchen to make it look as if no one had been there and settled back into the couch. She dialed Bo's number finally, and Marty picked up.

"Yeah?" Marty said.

Sylvia cringed at the sound of Marty's voice and immediately felt desperate for calling so late. She was smarter than this. She had to be careful. Bo was skittish but, after years of eye rolls, Marty seemed to be warming up to her. She had come to Sylvia for advice about the dance: that was new. Sylvia couldn't remember another time when Marty had asked her opinion about anything or had actually listened. She often waved *blah-blah-blah* when Sylvia was monologuing. Crazy how a child could make you feel like shit without ever opening her mouth.

But something had changed. Marty was acting different, maybe growing up. Recognizing, for a change, all that Sylvia could offer her. All that Sylvia *had* offered her over the years. She wasn't trying to replace her mother. Glory had been her best friend. They'd been inseparable since first grade. Called twins until it was clear to everyone that Glory was becoming beautiful, exceptionally so, while Sylvia was Sylvia. Even her parents called her *the sidekick*. And, well, that was fine with her.

What people didn't understand was that Glory had chosen Sylvia. They hadn't just been thrown together. Their houses weren't even close. Sylvia had grown up in a modest ranch in Red Cliff, while Glory had had her pick of rooms in a twelve-room Victorian, the historic Chateau overlooking Chequamegon Bay. It didn't matter that Glory was demanding, that she intimidated their teachers and classmates. She wasn't bad. She was charming. You should've heard her voice, seen that look in her eye. One minute you were the only person in the world who mattered, and the next you were nothing. A sack of potatoes.

Sylvia had been the only one capable of managing Glory, her mood swings, her sadness, which was perceived as her being standoffish, a snob. No one understood what she had been through. The prettier you were, the more problems you had—at least that's what Sylvia assumed.

The boys were terrible. The men, especially fathers, were worse.

Sylvia had soothed Glory while she sat weeping in bathroom stalls. Sylvia had protected her, had loved her to the point of wondering if she were actually in love.

But you can't love a person who only loves herself. Ask Bo. They had been through the same thing, weathered the same storm that was Glory and her ego. Her unhappiness was all-consuming. Her problems were yours to keep. In fact, she had given them to Sylvia.

Bo and Marty were her responsibility now. Babysitting while Bo worked long hours, and freezing casseroles and carting laundry to her basement. Hiding liquor and driving him to AA when he lost his license. The first few years after Glory left, things were bad.

Now Sylvia felt they were finally turning a corner. Bo was sober, giving her an ounce of attention, and Marty had come to her for help.

Sylvia had to be careful. One wrong move—acting too eager, like the other women; seeming desperate, which she was, hence the phone call at this hour—and Marty would be gone again.

Marty huffed into the receiver, annoyed. "Hello? I can hear you breathing."

Sylvia covered the phone with her hand.

"Mom?" Marty's voice softened. It was quiet, meek. "That you? Are you still in town?"

Sylvia jabbed the switch, hanging up.

Oh, God. Was Glory really back here after all these years? Had they been in touch? Was that even possible?

It was dark. Sylvia wrapped her arms around herself, digging her nails into her shoulders. Calm down. Glory wasn't here. Sylvia would've heard something. She would've seen her. Even if she hadn't yet seen her, she would've felt her presence as distinctly as rain pelting down on her skin, Sylvia caught in a downpour. That was the power of Glory. The whole town had revolved around her. She wasn't someone who could simply come back, after seven years of nothing, and go unnoticed. Everyone would be talking about her. Every chance encounter on the street would turn into an interrogation. *Where have you been?* Whatever answer she gave would ricochet from house to house. *Did you hear who's back in town?*

Glory Glory Glory.

Sylvia wanted to call Marty back. "Anything new?" she might say. "Anything you want to tell me?" Instead, she called every front-desk girl in the county, every sleazy highway motel. "I'm calling for Glory Olander, maiden name Vandehei." No, no, no. Before hanging up, one girl said, "I've heard stories about her."

Though it was getting late, Sylvia called Onie, Jaybird at the diner, old Iris from the bank, who was asleep when she called and spent most of the phone call describing a ridiculous dream. She even called her nemesis, Alice Lorrey. "I know this sounds crazy, but have you seen Glory? People are saying she's back in town."

There was silence on the other end.

"Alice, you awake? Have you seen her?"

Alice cleared her throat. "Lord, no." A strained laugh. "That would be bad for both of us, don't you think? Bad for every single woman, and there sure are a lot of us up here."

CHAPTER FOUR

Marta

Christmas came. There was a crooked tree, dragged in from the backyard. Dad stuck it in the corner of the living room. No lights, no tinsel. It sat there, dark and naked, shedding needles that pricked the bottoms of my feet. Finally, when the branches turned brown, he dragged it back outside and burned it in the fire pit. We didn't go anywhere on New Year's Eve, not to Jaybird's annual party with free Shirley Temples, five-buck prime rib, and a firework or two saved from the Fourth of July, set off from the roof.

Dad made Hamburger Helper without the hamburger, drank a forty of Schlitz ("One day lost is still seven years sober," he told me), and went to bed.

All winter break, he avoided me with odd jobs around the yard. Splitting wood. Knocking icicles from the gutter. Painting the house, though my mother was right, it didn't make any sense this time of year. During supper, when he couldn't avoid me any longer, I'd talk about Mom. Tell the story over. Ask the same questions. And each time he'd say that I'd been dreaming, that she hadn't come back and never would.

"What about the orange blossom?" I'd say, chasing him around the kitchen. The flower wasn't pretty anymore; it didn't smell like summertime. It was brown and sticky, a tar-colored mush. But it was real. That meant Mom was real, too. She had touched my hair. Laid beside me on the bed.

"If you're so sure she came back, then where is she?" Dad would say, glancing around the empty house.

"Maybe she left while I was sleeping."

"Why would she come back just to leave again?"

"I don't know. Maybe she was scared to see you."

My parents had fought before, seething looks and stretches of silence as long and harsh as a winter storm. They rarely yelled. Sometimes my mother would push my father, dig her nails into his forearm, bite his neck when he tried to kiss her.

"She wasn't scared of anything," he said.

"So you didn't hurt her? You didn't make her leave?"

"Jesus, Marty. Haven't you figured it out yet? She left a long time ago all on her own. She was the one who hurt *me*."

We kept arguing until Dad grew so tired he would barely answer. He'd dip his head back, blinking up at the ceiling, pinching his throat. He'd say things like "Your mother only loved herself," "She hated this place," and "You're crazy to think she'd ever come back."

But she had come back—I felt it—and I could feel her now. She was still here, sneaking through the cellar door at night, walking the halls in her high heels, touching banisters and maps and mildewed records we no longer played because of her; invading our dreams as Dad and I slept. Permanent as a name carved in a tree.

After school, I walked by every rental property in town: the one nice motel, a bunch of crummy motels, houses for rent, and every bungalow on the beach, hoping it were that easy, hoping I would glance through a window to find her there, her legs kicked up on the sofa, a gossip magazine splayed across her lap and the stereo turned up—Cyndi Lauper or Stevie Nicks. But it was winter and, apart from a few tourists, every room was empty.

After town, I crossed the ice road back to the island. I made a list of every place Mom had ever taken me: Big Bay State Park, the Island Inn, the history museum, the dump, the huge sprawling summer homes that were only used for a weekend. I went everywhere. I even broke a window at one of the summer homes and climbed into a bedroom, where I found the biggest closet I had ever seen. Clothes hanging in white garment bags like ghosts. I tried on a pair of heels, too big. I dug my bare feet into the soft white carpet. It was amazing how warm it was in there; they must've paid for heating year round. My mother had grown up like this. Heat. Garment bags. A walk-in closet. She belonged here.

Search the town. Then the island. This became my ritual.

At first, Dad tried to protest. When would I give this up? Didn't I have friends to see? Schoolwork?

"No friends." And I always did my homework during lunch.

He fixed his eyes on the floor. "Look, Marty. You can try all you want, but you're not going to find her." He said he had already called around. Talked to old friends and distant relatives. Apparently, nobody knew where she was. Nothing to go on. The sheriff's office couldn't even help. Well, maybe they could have, but they wouldn't. When I'd called to report a missing person, the cranky operator sighed into the phone. "Glory, huh?" she said, all nasal and annoyed. "Honey, people aren't missing when they leave on their own."

When I tried to explain, she sighed. "Honey, is your father there? Put him on." I hung up. I couldn't really trust him. In a town where everyone seemed to love him and hate my mother, I couldn't trust anyone.

Up in the lookout, I sat with Dad's binoculars pinned against the window, searching for a flicker of Mom's pink coat, those too-tan nylons, her yellow curls. The night was too full to see much of anything. Above me, a lonely moon. Below, an opossum sifting through the trash. I moved from window to window. Stopped to blow warm air into my hands. Pressed my face to the glass, fogged it up, and looked again.

Nothing.

Minutes felt like hours. I was bored and I was hungry. I ran through my options: Hungry-Man XXL. The guy who looked like a great dad, Chef Boyardee.

Something smacked the window.

My first thought was a bird. Crows were scary smart—I didn't like how they craned their heads to study me—but the robins, now that was a different story. I'd found plenty of dead robins lying on their backs, feet in the air like they were ready for bed.

Downstairs I could hear Dad rummaging around. Maybe finally making dinner.

It was quiet outside. I could see the silhouette of branches, black and reaching. The opossum, my only friend, was long gone.

Another crack, so hard the window shook. Not a bird. A rock.

I grabbed my flashlight and ran downstairs. I opened the front door quietly like those television detectives and slinked down the porch, flashlight off.

The woods were black. The night was heavy, closing in on us. I knew that whoever was out there could see me—they knew I couldn't see them.

"Who's there?" I said, feeling foolish. I was raised in the woods. Come morning this place would be as familiar as my bedroom, the pine trees dusting the sky, the sunlight scattered on the snow, warming the top of my head.

Something sharp hit my thigh.

In a swooping frenzy, I switched the flashlight on, wheeling it around the house.

Nothing.

No one.

Below me, square between my feet, a sharp red rock.

Maybe it was Mom smirking in the dark, her pink pockets full of sandstone skippers. "Glory." It was first time I'd used her name. I'd meant to sound mean, but it came out like a question.

Another one smacked my ankle.

There were footsteps, the rush of branches, the soft crunch of fresh snow, a snickering laugh. A man's voice. Much softer than my father's.

And then this low, mournful cry.

I dropped the flashlight, ran from the woods, up the porch, and there was Levi, leaning cool against the door.

"I got you good." He held a loon whistle like a piccolo.

I slugged his arm. "Thanks a lot." What I wanted to say was that he was crazy for coming here, that my dad knew of his reputation. Levi wasn't drinking or smoking weed like the other boys. He was banned from the library for writing "obscene" messages in romance novels: "Owls don't have eyeballs," "Red foxes wave their tails to say hey to other foxes," "Black bears are considered promiscuous."

That same year, he was suspended for two weeks for letting all of Mr. Purdy's soon-to-be dissected crayfish go free. Levi had stolen them from the class aquarium and released them into the icy lake where they died within minutes. "Frozen, wasted," Mr. Purdy had muttered after discovering the empty aquarium. "Louisiana crayfish special-ordered from the South."

Despite the crayfish tragedy of 1997, everybody had hated to see Levi go, especially Marianne and Chelsea, who had ranked him as "No. 3 hottie" for his Johnny Depp eyes—they were sad, beautiful, a sulking Gilbert Grape.

With Levi standing in front of me, his proud, smirking face catching the shallow light above the front door, I remembered just how right Marianne and Chelsea were, how jealous I had been when they'd baked him scotcheroos after he was suspended ("a noble rescue," they had called the crayfish release, despite the outcome), and why exactly I had said yes when he asked me to the dance. I leaned back against the porch rail, trying to seem cool. "What are you doing here?"

"You've been ditching me. Haven't seen you after school."

"I've been busy."

"You don't seem busy now."

"You got a great plan or something? You can't come inside, and I'm not sitting out here."

"I've got the ice boat. I can take you anywhere you want."

I smiled. "Why would I want to go anywhere with you?"

He paused. "We could look for your mom." Before I could say *I'm not looking*, he added, "I heard you say her name. You thought it was her in the woods."

Just like everyone else, he knew she'd left me. But he didn't know how much I wanted to find her now. And she could be anywhere. Including mine, there were twenty-two islands offshore, scattered like thumbprints. Islands without roads or people. Islands with a thousand places to hide. It seemed impossible to guess where my mother might be. The only place I could think to start was Devil's Island, a rocky heap of land surrounded by sea caves so deep and hollow they produced constant thunder. Because of the thunder, some believed the island was cursed, home to an evil spirit.

Devil's Island, my mother's favorite. Fitting, Dad always said.

———————

Levi's iceboat was an orange Mini Skeeter from the eighties, with three skates and a seat for one. It reminded me of a little racecar or a twin engine. During a semester's art class, he had painted a mural on the sail: a giant crayfish holding a Red Cliff flag. *The Freedom Flier*, she was called. He would race it one day; he would be sponsored by the casino. But for now, he was learning. When I said, "Is this even safe?," he smiled.

It was a short walk to the dock, which was deserted at this hour. The wind coming off the lake was brutal. Already, my eyes were watering. I hopped down from the dock, onto the seat of the boat, and waited as Levi climbed behind it and shoved as hard as he could.

Soon enough, the wind caught the sails, and the boat lurched forward. Levi leaped in, his side pressing into me, and we took off, straight into nothing. Total darkness for miles and miles, apart from the light of the moon and the lighthouse in the distance, too far to see from my house. It was only visible out here on the frozen lake, which could give way any moment. I imagined the ice cracking beneath us. Swallowing us like a giant taking a big gulp. Sinking slowly and then all at once—completely underwater. There was no moon now. There was only black and the shock of that water, like a thousand needles. Or maybe it would feel like nothing. Like you were already dead.

In reality, our journey was slow-going, anticlimactic. We were gliding over the ice. The scraping of the skates was fairly quiet. And instead of sinking, we occasionally took flight— whenever we hit a snowdrift. *The Freedom Flier* actually felt freeing. Wind in my hair. That sensation of flying, really flying, lifting off, out of here.

I felt good and then really angry thinking of my mother leaving. Feeling this light and this good and this willing to trade everything for the unknown. It could've been hell out there. Crummy jobs and trailer parks: not the nice ones; the grimy, dilapidated ones where the poorest kids lived. *Remember that next time you're complaining about the hot water*, Dad would say whenever we drove past them.

I never got the sense Mom had something waiting on the other side. She had taken off into the darkness, just like us. No direction. No end goal or dreams, none that she spoke of, not that Dad or Sylvia knew. Seven years ago she must've walked down our driveway, tasting a little hint of freedom. It must've carried her forward, that wind in her hair, until she was so far away that she forgot we were here.

It took longer than expected to reach Devil's Island, but there it was, the flashing red lighthouse, which sat high upon the cliffs. Levi steered us toward the dock carefully, more slowly than I could stand, on account of those cliffs and the sea caves beneath them.

I was no longer worried about how dangerous this was. Dad would have lost his mind if he'd known I was this far away, eighteen miles, in the middle of the night. I had no idea how late it was, how many hours had gone by. I just knew I was cold. I wanted to curl up and sleep, but we had to keep moving. Out of the boat, onto the dock, and then, using Levi's flashlight, into the sea caves, which bellowed from the wind.

Nightmarish icicles hung from the ceiling, sharp as daggers. I didn't look up as I walked below them. Deeper and deeper into the caves, dead quiet. No wind, no nothing. I made fists inside my mittens to keep my fingers from going numb.

We climbed up to the island into the black woods. For miles, we pushed through packing snow, knee deep, our faces slick with sweat and freezing. Every now and then, we heard a sharp crack—a branch giving way to snow. No matter where you were in the woods, it felt like someone was right behind you.

I wanted to believe it was her. I knew I should say something. *Hello? Anyone?* Call her name, let it echo through the woods, into the caves like thunder. But I was too embarrassed. Afraid that Levi would think this was all some joke, an excuse for the two of us to sneak out. *This isn't a date*, I wanted to say. Then why was I acting so weird, silent, nervous? Why was I thinking of excuses to leave? *It's too cold.* I was sweating. *Dad will be worried.* Or drunk. *The sun will be up soon.*

But here was the lighthouse. Out of nowhere, it sprang up like a rocket ship, beckoning us forward.

"I've seen bigger," Levi said, hanging onto a smirk.

There was a sound—soft, like humming.

"Do you hear that?" I said.

"Are you trying to scare me? It's working."

"Listen."

We shoved through the snow, closer, closer. And then we could hear it. The crack of static. A song coming from the highest window. REO Speedwagon's "Keep on Loving You." It was one of Dad's favorites.

Levi was beaming. "We have to go up."

"It's probably locked."

"Scared?"

"Yeah, right."

"Maybe your mom's up there."

"It's not her."

"How do you know?"

"Because." I felt myself sinking in the snow. "She would never play this song."

"So it's the lighthouse keeper."

"There hasn't been one for years."

I watched him wade through the snow. He grabbed the door handle and leaned back, using the weight of his body. To our surprise, the door cracked open. Before I could say anything, he slipped inside. The door thudded closed, and it was just me out there. Me and whoever was watching.

"It's empty," he called from the window. "Somebody left the radio on."

I made my way up the spiral stairs and into the watch. It was a circular room with warped wood paneling and a long convex window, all of it lake, seemingly endless, no matter which way you looked. There wasn't much in the room: a couple of life rings hanging from nails, a hurricane of a bookshelf, and a small wooden desk in the corner with a dusty radio and a package of powdered donuts that had expired in 1995, three years ago.

"Hungry?" Levi poked the donuts. They were still soft, and I was hungry but not that hungry. "These are like McDonald's hamburgers. They never go bad." He sat down at the desk as if it were his own and started flipping through radio stations. The sound was mostly static, one chanting from the rez.

He returned to the one station that came in clear: alt rock. Another song I recognized, "Dumb" by Nirvana, the outro repeating the same phrase over and over, like it was meant for me.

My mother was not here.

She would've never come here in the dead of winter. Why come back at all? Just to look at us, to laugh at the blistering paint, at my tangled hair? Laugh and leave again? Maybe there was another family. Another daughter in the Gulf of Mexico. Not boyish and pale, average in every subject. An island freak. No, she was the kind of girl people looked at. Pretty and blonde like Marianne and Chelsea. Clever and kind with little jokes and straight white teeth.

For the first time everything became clear, as glaring as the beacon on the ice below: Dad wasn't the only reason she'd left. It was me.

Though it was cold enough to see my breath, my face burned. I could feel the sweat on my neck, under Mom's heavy mink coat. I could feel the weight of Levi's eyes on me. That sweet, suffering expression. Like he knew what I was thinking. That I had just realized what everyone in town already knew: my mother did not love me. She was gone and so what? Half the kids in town had single parents. It was usually the dads who left.

I pressed my hand against the convex window, leaving a mark. Down below you could see the cliffs, sheer and red and empty. Fifty feet to the water. Mom had jumped from this very spot. I had found the picture inside Dad's old Tom Petty record. The picture was dated July 4, 1981. My mother would have been seventeen. She wore a white high-cut bikini. Her whole body was suspended in the air, her yellow hair raised all around her like a misapplied halo. She was smiling at the camera. There could've been huge jagged rocks beneath her or the kind of sand you melt into. You aim for the right spot, but you never really knew. So much hidden beneath the surface of the lake and behind her smile.

Levi turned up the radio—"Eternal Flame" by The Bangles.

He grabbed the walkie-talkie and sang into it like a microphone. He was smirking that big smirk. Somehow not embarrassed; that was just how he was.

His voice was sweeter than I'd imagined. Sweet and low. I had heard the song a million times, but it sounded different the way he was singing it. Less like a love song. More one-sided.

I must've looked sad. I must've sucked all the energy from the room because his smile dropped. "You want to go home? I shouldn't have dragged you out here."

There was no reason to stay. The air was musty and cold, and it was only getting colder. It would be brutal walking out of here and sinking back into the freezing iceboat. Bearing the wind and the weight of my own stupidity, having come all this way for nothing.

"Can we stay?" I asked, wishing I could maroon myself forever. There was nothing here for me, and there was nothing back home.

His eyes brightened. "Of course." He was being too nice, like everyone had been after Mom had left. "We can stay as long as you want."

"I'll sleep here," he added, a joke, but he definitely would.

I stood there like an idiot feeling sorry for myself. I didn't know what to say.

"My mom went to school with your mom," he said.

"Surprising in a town this big." Even in a bad mood, I was capable of sarcasm.

"Ha-ha." Levi shook his head. "I mean they were in the same class. They were friends."

I braced myself for what might come next. I had heard all kinds of stories. People seemed to like to tell me how bad she was, how snooty, how they'd never liked her—not ever!—as if it were a comfort to me. Like suddenly I'd believe them when they told me, "You're better off."

"They lined up their schedules junior year. Skipped a lot

of class under the guise of an independent study." He used air quotes, and we both laughed. "Something I would do."

"To be honest I don't know a whole lot about her."

"My mom has pictures, a journal they passed back and forth. Mostly dumb stuff, about guys. There's a whole passage about your dad. They both liked him."

"Everyone does." I rolled my eyes. There was Sylvia, Marianne's mom, the woman at the Burger King twenty miles down the highway, and of course my teachers and tourists and old grannies that sat like fixtures in the diner, admiring him.

"My mom said I can give it to you if you want. The journal." He glanced up at me. He looked like he might cry. "She wants to meet you."

"Who?"

"My mom."

I had only ever seen Levi's mom, Laura, from a distance. She was intimidating—long dark hair, gun at her hip. She was the game warden. His father was the one who stayed home, doing God knows what, like my dad.

"I don't know." I didn't feel comfortable talking to parents. Or anyone.

"At least take the journal." He reached into the inner pocket of his thick corduroy jacket and pulled out the journal. Pocket-sized, worn, spiral-bound. He had been holding onto it this whole time. He knew more about my mom than I did.

I could feel my body tensing up. I could feel that golf ball in the back of my throat. I wanted him to push me, like Dad had done during our worst fights, so that I could hit him back. I could shove him off this lighthouse. But before I knew it, he had wrapped his arms around me. His breath was hot on the top of my head. He was saying, "I'm sorry, I'm sorry, Marty," and it was then that I realized I was crying. "Forget about the journal."

But it wasn't the journal I cared about. I could read it or not, and it wouldn't matter. It wouldn't change the one thing that had brought me here.

My mother was gone.

It didn't matter if I found her. If she came back once or a hundred times because she was never really *here*.

It was still dark outside when I returned to the house. Dad was gone. For the next few weeks, he ignored me like the growing heap of dirty laundry at the bottom of the stairs. Probably thinking I was just like my mother—a runaway, a good-for-nothing girl.

Her journal sat unopened on my nightstand. Just looking at it made me angry. This was exactly what she would have wanted, me reading the journal, obsessing over her every thought, trying to make sense of it. Who was my mother?

Nothing more than a ghost-white garment bag in a big empty house.

CHAPTER FIVE

Sylvia

Sylvia pushed her withdrawal slip beneath the teller window, and old Iris frowned at the amount. "I shouldn't be saying nothing." This was something Iris always said. "But I'm worried. 'Course I am. I know how hard ya work. And we know how much ya make, how much Lansky charges for rent. Heating alone, shame on him." She leaned forward like she was about to whisper but didn't. "Just thought I should say it in case no one else does. You're losing, hey? And don't I know where it's going."

"That so?" Sylvia was prepared for this. Iris was a gossip. Had been for fifty years. She didn't really know where Sylvia's money was going. Occasionally, Sylvia made checks out to Bo (the whole town knew she pined for him), but the rest was done in cash. This time, she needed $65.

Iris licked her thumb and counted the bills.

"For Onie, if ya have ta know," Sylvia said, mimicking Iris's thick Yooper accent. "Wait till I leave before ya run and tell de other girls."

Another teller, a teenage girl who was eavesdropping, snickered into her big computer screen. "She got you there."

Sylvia didn't look back, but she could feel Iris seething. Boring a hole into her back.

It was cold outside but warm for February. Sylvia opened her mouth, letting a few fat snowflakes fall onto her tongue. For the first time in years, she felt young, full of possibility.

Everything was coming together for Marty's birthday. Bo had called Sylvia—he called her—with a gift idea. Something of Glory's that needed to be fixed up. Sylvia had already made the arrangements with Onie, and now there was nothing left to do but make the cake. A tricky recipe. Sifting. Separating. Frosting. Piping. A chore really, but Marty loved it.

Sylvia's joy lasted so long into the day that when Lars called, she told him she was busy. She worked the night shift at Jaybird's dreaming of the birthday party. When she had turned thirteen, her parents had been out of town. There was no cake, no party, but Glory was there. She had given Sylvia a short gold necklace with a white arrowhead. "Sugar quartz," Glory said. "Rare, you know. Very. I could've kept it for myself." She swept Sylvia's hair aside and hooked the arrowhead around her neck. "But it's pretty on you," she said, petting the stone. "And now you'll think of me every time you wear it."

It was painful now, remembering how close they'd been. Glory had treated Sylvia like an extension of herself, and what a wonderful thing to be, an extension of that beauty. To walk arm in arm with the most popular girl in school. To be the one she loved and confided in, even if she was mean, which she was. But, oh, when her eyes landed on you!

Sylvia scrubbed the floors, the counters, the malt machine, trying to force that memory from her mind. Glory was a million miles away. Gone. And so was the necklace. Chucked from Sylvia's apartment window about a month after Glory had left. Glory was supposed to call from a motel or payphone every Sunday evening to let Sylvia know where she was. After a month of nothing, Glory mailed a cocktail napkin that said, "Sylvie, darling. Send me something." On the backside, she left an address. No "thanks."

Sylvia dropped her rag into the wash bin and pushed through the swinging doors, into the back. She opened the walk-in freezer and stood there, letting the cold pour over her body. Her upper lip was lined with sweat, her bra sticky and digging into her ribs. She wanted to take her clothes off. Lie naked in the freezer until her mind was numb. *Don't think about Glory. Don't.*

There would be a birthday party. Potato-chip casserole. The surprise gift. Cards after cake. Late-night television. Reruns of *The Twilight Zone*, Marty's favorite. Marty would fall asleep on the couch. Bo would smile. Lean a little closer to Sylvia. Spend the night. Maybe. If she were lucky. Though she didn't believe in God, she crossed herself and prayed for it.

CHAPTER SIX

Marta

Ever since Mom left, Sylvia insisted on throwing me birthday parties and, each year, just a day or two before, I wished we'd both catch a nasty cold. This time, I couldn't avoid her. Dad said we had to go, that thirteen was special. It didn't feel special, but Dad seemed excited, and I didn't want to disappoint him again.

At Sylvia's apartment, they sang "Happy Birthday" badly, like everyone does. I smiled, pretending to enjoy myself. I didn't think of Mom's face, painted and pretty, all over Sylvia's apartment in "Friendship" picture frames and photo books. I didn't think of Sylvia's hand, her nails a burning fire-engine red, wrapped around Dad's leg beneath the glass table. I blew out thirteen candles, wishing it would all be over soon.

The birthday cake was strawberry with pink piped flowers. "Chrysanthemums," Sylvia said. "Your own piece of summertime."

Though I hated strawberry and couldn't stand the pink, I ate a big slice and applauded her petal work. It was like something from Betty Crocker. It must've taken all afternoon.

"So what'd you wish for?" Sylvia smiled, probably thinking of a boy. She squeezed Dad's leg.

I wished for a bear to break through the front door and chomp off your hand. For a chocolate cake with chocolate frosting. For blue chrysanthemums or, better yet, none at all because it was March and sugar flowers, no matter how great the petals were, did not bring back summertime.

"I wished for a popup tent. And my own pair of binoculars."

Sylvia frowned at the present she had wrapped for me. It

was a square box with pink glittered wrapping paper and a giant gold bow.

Dad scooped up a second piece of cake and dumped it onto his plate. "Don't worry, she'll love it." He smiled at Sylvia. "No one knows Marty better than you."

I flattened a chrysanthemum with my fork.

She certainly knew me better than Dad did since he really didn't know a thing. He only asked generic questions like "How was school?" if he bothered to ask at all. Sylvia, on the other hand, wouldn't stop talking. My earliest memories included hanging out at the diner, overhearing conversations between her and Mom, both of them going a mile a minute.

Even after Mom left, I went to the diner every day. Sylvia could talk about anything and nothing. She liked helping me with homework; she was only good at math. She wanted specifics about my friends, which I would often make up on account of not having them.

Sylvia was a fountain of knowledge, a repository of gossip. She knew everyone's personal history, as if, in addition to waitressing, that was her job. The only things I knew about my parents from before I was born were the things she told me. How they first started dating, even though Sylvia was the one that liked him. How they stole Grandpa Jan's '63 Corvette and hit a deer that same night. How they loved each other silently, barely saying a word.

Sylvia had been there at the wedding, holding Mom's baby's breath and fixing her train. Following her around like her "personal servant." She had been there during the arguments, the many times Mom had left in the middle of the night. And, of course, Sylvia had been there when Mom left for good. Sylvia moved into our lives swiftly like an understudy stepping into her role.

I shoved the mashed frosting into my mouth and smiled at the narrow space between Dad and Sylvia. "Dad's right. Whatever it is, I'll love it. I always do."

Last year, it had been a horrific Lisa Frank notebook with a smiling, bright-white polar bear cub on the cover. A girl cub— you could tell by the purple eyelashes—playing with a bunch of rainbow-colored penguins, who looked totally at ease with the bear. One of them was even laughing as he flew overhead. *Not very accurate.* The next day in school, after I'd gingerly pulled the notebook from my desk, Chelsea practically jumped out of her seat. She had her own Lisa Frank with two large penguins hugging on a lone iceberg. We were soul sisters, Chelsea had cried to the whole eighth-grade class. Soul sisters for the rest of the afternoon. Sylvia had meant well, though. She hadn't known that Chelsea's mother had a similar taste in "Arctic Friends."

Years before, it had been a manicure set. "For your nails," Sylvia had explained. When I got home from my party, I dumped the clear plastic bag onto my bed. "You could kill a pheasant with something like that," Dad had said, gesturing to the file.

Sylvia knew me better than anyone, but on birthdays she tried to give me the things she would've liked herself at that age, things my mother would've loved. There were little graphic t-shirts ("Girl Power," "Talk to the Hand") and babydoll dresses to replace the overalls I wore, shiny platform sneakers to replace my signature (secondhand) Doc Martens, which I almost never took off, only to shower. It wasn't that I hated the clothes. It was more that I didn't need them, only on special occasions, like all-you-can-eat pancakes after mass with Grandma Lotte and Grandpa Jan before they died and during parent-teacher conferences.

I couldn't imagine what kind of girlie thing she had wrapped up this time. Whatever it was, it was big. Maybe a foot spa or the BeDazzler I'd seen on infomercials. I could tell you one thing, it was definitely not a tent or a pair of binoculars. Sylvia was not the kind of woman who went camping, though she might've tried to appear outdoorsy to please Dad.

Just as she would do in the diner, Sylvia cleared the table, balancing three plates, half a cake, a can of whipped cream, and a handful of forks all the way to the kitchen, hips swinging.

Dad watched her leave and come back.

Sylvia stood before me, hiding the present behind her back, though I'd already seen it. "You ready?" Her eyes lit up like it was her own birthday.

I ran my fingers along the plastic table covering, feeling the sticky surface. She was waiting for me to say there was nothing I was looking forward to more.

"Come on, Marty." Dad held up the Polaroid camera. "I'll get your reaction on tape."

My fingertips were sticky with frosting. I half-smiled at Sylvia so Dad could take the picture she was hoping for, the picture she would hang with the others on the fridge, a row of happy birthdays from six until now.

The wrapping paper felt coarse as sandpaper. Years later, I would remember this feeling. The rough glitter, the weight of the box, more substantial than a Lisa Frank, the hush of the living room. I ripped at the bow and tore into the paper with convincing enthusiasm, enough to make Sylvia lean in close, hovering, a strand of her red hair dusting my shoulder.

It was a plain white hatbox. I lifted the lid and parted a rainbow of tissue paper. Inside, a heap of blue. I pulled at the pile until the fabric unfolded like a paper note taking its proper form. A dress. Blue slippery chiffon with a ruffled neckline and a long, blooming skirt. Exactly like the one Mom had given me but with a ton of sequins, like a night sky across the skirt.

Dad snapped a picture, and the Polaroid spilled out into the quiet room.

"Well?" There was panic in her voice.

I brought the dress up to my face. Lilac. The smell of open windows in the summertime.

"Onie added sequins, just how you like." Sylvia grabbed the dress and held it up to her body. "Here," she said, sashaying toward her bedroom. "Come try it on."

"My dress." I wanted to rip it from her hands. "You have it."

"Marty," Dad cut in.

Sylvia came back to the table and sat hugging the dress. "Don't you like it? Don't you want to go to the dance? I talked to your daddy. He's gonna let you go."

Dad said nothing. He was watching the Polaroid develop. I could see the faded, ghostly outline of my face, the awful stare. He saw it, too, and flipped the photo over.

"Aren't you happy?" She held out the dress. When I grabbed it from her, the tulle snagged on her finger.

"Where'd you get this?" I asked.

"You're mad? No, Marty, you don't understand. This was your mother's dress. She wore it to our first high school dance. Homecoming, must have been."

"Why do you have it?"

"I found it at the house."

"When were you at our house?"

Sylvia blushed. "The other day."

"You went through Mom's stuff?"

"Don't blame Sylvia. The dress was my idea. You were looking for Mom. I thought it would help, having her dress. Stupid idea."

I turned back to Sylvia. "Where did you find it?"

Her face was as red as her hair. "In the bedroom, under the bed."

"Mom gave me this dress. You took it from her."

"Took it?" Sylvia bit her bottom lip. "Your father asked me to."

Dad and Sylvia were in on something. They had taken the dress and sent Mom away. I didn't know whose idea it was or why they were coming together after all these years.

"You ruined it. The sequins weren't meant for this dress. This dress was perfect."

"I don't know what to say." That was a first. "I made a mistake, I guess, going through her things." She pushed out from the table, scurried to her room.

"Sylvia," Dad called.

She closed the door.

Dad hung his head. "You wanted a dress. You been asking to go to a dance."

"That was before Mom disappeared."

"Marty, she didn't disappear."

"Then where is she?"

He hesitated, his thumb pressed against his throat. "She wasn't back in the first place."

"You used to fight with her. She used to crawl into bed with me some nights. I bet she's afraid of you. I bet she'd come back again if you left."

"You want me to leave?"

"Why don't you move in with Sylvia? She wants you to."

He jerked his thumb toward the door. "Go wait outside."

"So you can be alone with her?"

"Listen. Can you hear that, Mother Teresa? She's crying, and it's because of you."

Dad left me at the table, and I sat there listening. It didn't bother me at all, hearing her cry like a little mouse.

CHAPTER SEVEN

Marta

"Marty, come on. We're going to be late."

As punishment for my behavior at Sylvia's, Dad didn't ground me or send me to the diner with fake flowers and a fake apology. He did something much worse.

Somehow, he'd managed to get a winter renovating job on the mainland, over at Alice Lorrey's Victorian, which also happened to be Marianne's house. Mrs. Lorrey had commissioned a new bedroom for her daughter because the school year had been "especially trying for Marianne." Her grade had dropped to an A- in algebra, and she hadn't gotten onto the ballot for homecoming (it was "all politics!"). The best part of the deal, Dad relayed sheepishly, was that Mrs. Lorrey had offered—no, insisted—on throwing me a late birthday party when the renovations were done. A princess-themed slumber party with makeovers for all the girls. "Would Marta like to wear a tiara?" she'd asked.

Absolutely, Dad had told her, getting even in the worst way he could.

I was not ready. I had not showered for a few days at least. I hunkered down on the couch and turned the TV all the way up.

He snatched the remote. Clicked *off*. "If this goes well, Mrs. Lorrey might have another job for me. She said something about the bathrooms, retiling a shower. Funny how rich people can't find better things to do with their money."

"We don't need their money."

He laughed.

"Not this much."

His smile faded. "Yes. We do."

"For what?"

He jammed his hands into his pockets.

"Dad?" I was angry now.

"Nothing, nothing," he kept saying to himself. "Well, the house."

"The house?"

"I've got a few bills. You know how winters are tough."

"You really need the work?" We'd never really talked about money, but I wasn't stupid. I knew my dad barely worked. I figured that had been one of the reasons Mom had left.

"Please don't look at me like that. Yes, I need the work." His eyes were big and pleading. It made me sad, seeing him like this, practically begging, like I had a choice.

When Dad wanted to seem fancy, he borrowed the neighbor's truck, a junky pickup with squawking doors and a hissing heater that spat out dust. He'd been borrowing it for the past few weeks, pleased as punch to be driving it through town. Even more pleased that Mrs. Lorrey probably thought we owned it, had assumed he'd gotten his license back.

The Lorreys' Victorian looked like a gingerbread house, too neat to be real. The whole thing was set off from town: three stories, a replica playhouse in the backyard, wild lupines blanketed with clean blue tarps, the stately gazebo, and the swimming pool that was closed for ten months of the year. In elementary school, during show-and-tell, Marianne would bring in pictures of her house as if we hadn't already seen it. She delighted in telling stories of how tourists would stop by, thinking they had stumbled upon a stranded piece of Disneyland.

Before I had a chance to get out of the truck, Mrs. Lorrey came rushing out of the house, her hair still set in rollers, a red velvet dress stretched tight across her hips.

"Greetings, Marta," she said through the closed passenger window, her smile aggressive and wide. A smudge of purple lipstick on her front teeth.

Dad leaned across me to roll down the window, a dozen hard cranks in the freezing cold. As the glass escaped the frame, I found myself face to face with Mrs. Lorrey and her lipstick. She curled her fingers around the edge of the window and leaned as far as she could into the truck.

"I've heard so much about you." She nodded back at the house. "The girls are inside."

"Sorry for the curlers." She touched the rollers on her head and plucked out a few pins, letting her highlighted hair tumble down, a bubble of bangs. She was as beautiful as a news anchor.

"I like your dress." It felt like something I should say.

She pushed herself off the car and did a slow turn, pausing to peer back at us.

"She used to be a pageant queen," Dad said. "Back in Georgia." Normally, I would've thought it was strange, him knowing something like that. But you could just tell.

We clapped for her, this little mannequin come to life, and she beamed back at us. She trotted over to Dad's window this time, and he cranked it open.

"You have to come inside," she said through the growing gap. "It's beautiful."

"I'll take your word for it, Mrs. Lorrey." Dad smiled without teeth.

"Alice, just Alice." She leaned through the window, getting really close, like it was just the two of them. My cue to leave.

I popped the door and grabbed my backpack. "See you tomorrow."

Dad put the truck in reverse and started backing up with Mrs. Lorrey's fingers still holding onto the window. "Okay, now. Have fun."

Mrs. Lorrey and I watched as the truck dipped down the hill and started across the lake.

"Here, Marty—I can call you Marty, right?" She trotted toward me. "We'll absolutely freeze to death out here. Let's go on in."

Inside, I was met by my own face, twice its real size, on a huge swooping banner: "Happy (Late) Birthday, Princess." The photo was a class picture of me from the fourth grade, a massive diamond tiara magically added to the top of my head. In the picture, I was smiling but not. My new bangs had been cut straight across but were too short and angled like a wheelchair ramp. It had been my first school picture after Mom left. Dad had let me wear a pair of acid-washed overalls and had decided it would be easier ("more economical") to cut my hair himself.

"Do you like it? It's the only photo Marianne had." Mrs. Lorrey squeezed my shoulder. "Oh, Marty, it's too cute. And the crown is right where it belongs."

She ushered me through the entryway, past abandoned sneakers, backpacks, and poorly rolled sleeping bags, into the sitting room, which was something like a living room but fancier: vaulted ceiling, family portrait (four children—where were they?) above the fireplace, a couch that looked like it had never been sat on.

Every girl from class was already here, six bored-looking girls in flare jeans and t-shirts—I was the only one in a dress—and black chokers. Half of the girls were on the couch; the others nestled below them, their heads tucked between knees, getting their hair crimped or braided. The center coffee table was covered with presents. I couldn't imagine unwrapping each one, having to smile and thank them for mini nail polishes, chokers like theirs, and games that were meant to be played with your family.

Marianne popped up from the sofa.

"Happy birthday." She grabbed my hand and led me across the room. "I told my mom that princess parties were for sixth-grade babies. It's totally embarrassing. You should see my new room." Marianne rolled her eyes and plopped down on the floor, tugging my hand to make me sit. "You can go now, Mom," she said, no longer diplomatic.

Mrs. Lorrey nodded at Marianne, an obedient smile, and left for the kitchen.

Marianne held court. "Meeting," she said.

Chelsea, Tiff, Rachel, Namid, and Winnie gathered on the floor around the coffee table, their faces pinched in annoyance. A quiet fell so we could only hear the Spice Girls playing on a distant boom box and Mrs. Lorrey washing dishes.

"We all know Marta doesn't like girly things. She doesn't listen to the Spice Girls. She doesn't do her hair, obviously. I'm not sure she even wanted to come. She avoids us, right? Like the plague."

I should've said something nice, tried to refute it, but she would see right through me.

Rachel worked her crimped-blonde hair into a high pony. "So why are we here?"

"Because she needs someone besides her dad to throw her a party. Thirteen is a big deal."

"Thirteen?" Namid scoffed. "You're only thirteen?"

"She's advanced," Marianne said.

"Advanced," Chelsea repeated dutifully.

"Oh, yeah," Tiff said, turning to me. "You started kindergarten early, right? I heard your mom begged the principal to let you in."

"I never heard that," Marianne said.

"Don't you remember? My dad was the head of the PTA. Her mom did a whole presentation, trying to prove Marta was super-smart, that she needed extra stimulation. But that wasn't true, no offense."

"Don't say that."

"Settle down, Mari. It's no big deal," Tiff said lazily, taking time to cross her legs. "Maybe my mom stuck around, but she didn't want to. I can tell. Some people aren't stoked about having kids."

Why had it taken me so long to understand what she had grasped so easily? The room grew hotter, more unbearable each time Tiff glanced at me. She was smiling casually, waiting for me to smile back. A few of the girls cleared their throats; one hummed along to the boom box. Marianne's face was twisted in frustration, bottom lip pinned beneath her straight front teeth.

"Anyway, I've got a tent in my room." She smiled at me. She was being kind, changing the subject. "You like tents, right?"

"Never had one."

"But you wish you did."

That stung.

Mrs. Lorrey came back with a tray of funfetti cupcakes. I thanked her for going to the trouble ("Box mix is no trouble," she said) and blew out the spiral trick candles until I was out of breath. Another thirteenth birthday.

Marianne instructed each girl to open a present on the coffee table for me. In order of reveal: hair crimper; No Doubt CD; red velvet dress like the one Mrs. Lorrey was wearing ("Don't worry," Marianne had said. "I have the gift receipt."); Girl Scout compass to make up for the dress; a used copy of *Harry Potter* I'd seen Rachel reading during study hall; and a pastel, multicolored scarf crocheted by Tiff's dad. He was the area's resident artist. "Another word for unemployed," my dad had said.

After Mrs. Lorrey went crazy with her big digital camera, we were finally allowed to go up to Marianne's bedroom. The door itself was painted lily-white with Marianne's name written in pretty purple cursive. Dad had told me it had taken him six tries to get the name right, starting, painting over it, waiting for the paint to set and dry, and trying again until Mrs. Lorrey signed off. I wasn't sure if she had mentioned to the girls that my father had done the work. They didn't say.

Before opening her bedroom door, Marianne offered me a sorry smile and kept smiling as the girls poured in. I was pitiful, embarrassed by her smile, ashamed that Dad had needed the work. But when I finally looked up into the sunny space of her bedroom, I felt a huge swell of admiration. Dad had carved flowers into the posts of her canopy bed—what looked like morning glories. You could see wrinkles in each petal, the tiny, delicate veins of each leaf.

As the girls gathered on Marianne's bed, sitting cross-legged and gushing about Teddy Bainbridge, the varsity pitcher, and his scandalously tight baseball pants, I walked around her room, touching the choreography of her pristine desk: the perfectly placed coffee cup and its gleaming circle of gel pens, the unopened diary in the center, and, near the edge, the framed picture of Marianne and a plump toddler. I ran my fingers along the bookshelf, along each dustless spine. There were trinkets: an antique music box, a seashell full of rhinestone earrings, a whole shelf of American Girl dolls, worth more than what Dad made in a month. I imagined my father painstakingly arranging them, fixing Felicity's bonnet, Addy's bow. Making this place perfect like he'd never done for me.

Though the tent was meant for two, we managed to squeeze all seven girls inside, a tight circle of knees and elbows. They were not into make-believe camping or makeovers. They had grown up into teenagers with boyfriends, second-to-third-base stories, and strategies for stuffing. Chelsea used tissues from the Kleenex box on Mr. Purdy's desk. Tiff used her big brother's thick hockey socks. Rachel and Winnie didn't need to stuff. Namid called them liars and tried to feel their chests. There was a commotion. A smashing of knees and elbows. Marianne told everyone to *please* shut up.

When the room grew dark, Tiff pulled a single grubby cigarette from her back pocket. "Can we?" she said.

Marianne ducked her head outside the tent, listening. "I think it's fine. Mom's probably reading one of her romance novels. My dad's been gone a lot."

"Where?" The first word I'd said in hours.

"So she *can* talk," Tiff said.

Marianne looked down at a small chip on her pink thumbnail. It was strange to see her hesitate. "He works in Duluth. Sometimes farther out of town. Like Manhattan—as in New York City—or Paris."

"As in France? Je pense que non," Tiff said, lighting up. She was ruthless.

The other girls tried not to laugh.

"You're doing it wrong." Namid snatched the cigarette. She took a long drag and exhaled without coughing. "Marta's turn."

Marianne cut in, "She doesn't have to."

Namid rolled her eyes. "Don't be a baby."

I took the cigarette.

"Don't be a bully," Marianne said to Namid.

And then to me: "Don't let anyone boss you around."

"Maybe she wants to." It was Chelsea joining in. "You don't have to be a loner, Marta. You can be like us."

I considered pitching the cigarette into Chelsea's shiny hair. Instead, I kissed the cigarette, now dewy from other mouths, and felt the hot-hot hiss of the paper. It tasted like a bonfire and burned like one too. I waited, and then I let the hurt blossom from my mouth. I coughed, but they cheered anyway, even Marianne.

"You're not supposed to inhale. Jesus," Tiff said. "She took it like a joint."

My head spun like a round on the Tilt-a-Whirl. Marianne stamped out the cigarette and ordered Chelsea to clear the haze. She flapped and flapped her arms around like a heavy Arctic penguin trying to take flight. I pushed all the knees and hands away from me and crawled through the door, into the open periwinkle of her room. It was dark. The girls' voices felt weak, far off. Marianne's nail polish came reaching after me, but I said, "I'm fine. I swear," and I zipped up the tent, snagging her arm. She screamed. I went into the hall and closed the door.

On the third floor of Marianne's house, there were two other bedrooms with blue walls and baseball decals: Louisville

Sluggers, Wilson gloves, and red-stitched baseballs, all pale gray in the dark. There were desks with empty drawers, only a stray sock left behind. The closets were empty, too, but the shelves were full of photographs and plastic trophies and rows of hanging medals. "MVP 1994," "Conference Champions," "Most Improved," they said, most of the ribbons royal blue to match the walls. The two bedrooms were identical to each other. Maybe they had belonged to Marianne's older brothers—twins, both baseball stars in high school before I was old enough to know. Marianne was a gossip, but I'd never heard her talk about them, hadn't heard the town talk about Mr. Lorrey and his disappearing job, his mysterious travels to Paris, or the half-empty, three-story Victorian.

I sat in one of the identical rooms, on some older brother's tightly made bed. I thought about slipping inside and waiting there until morning, silent, flat as I could lie against the mattress so they wouldn't know I was here.

There were other places to hide: the miniature playhouse, the gazebo, inside the drained swimming pool. I couldn't go back to the tent, and I couldn't go home. Dad might smell the rush of cigarettes in my hair. He would think of Mom, and that would be worse. Maybe better to hide in the bathtub, soak my head underwater until it was erased, until I was clean again.

Before I could move, the door handle twisted.

Mrs. Lorrey appeared in a short fluffy robe. "Marianne told me you feel sick." She looked genuinely sorry, like it was her fault. But it was—wasn't it?

She sat down beside me on the bed. "You know, I thought throwing you a princess party would keep you girls out of trouble, but you're not kids. Sometimes I forget what I was doing at your age." She pulled a pack of cigarettes from her robe and knocked one out. When she lit up, I could see her face more clearly, blank and quiet-looking without the makeup. I liked her better this way.

She took a drag and offered it to me. "I can keep a secret.

Marianne doesn't even know I smoke." She parted her thin, wiry lips, and smoke fell from her mouth.

"It makes me sick." I waved my hand in front of my face. "The smoke."

She got up and stamped the cigarette out on the trophy shelf. "Oh, don't worry. He won't notice. He doesn't come back here. It's not good for his 'depression.'" She used air quotes.

I knew this was a fancy word for sad. "Is he sick or something?"

"How you can you be sick when you have everything? I'm the one who needs help."

When we were young, these were the moments no one expected of us, no one expected children to bear—this sadness between adults, this desperation to be heard and comforted, to be complimented by your daughter's classmate's dad. I couldn't stand it. But here, in this empty room, Mrs. Lorrey demanded it. She was waiting, hunched over the forgotten shelf. Melodramatic, as if this were her scene, her time to shine, the movie star.

"So what happened?" I said.

She rushed back over to the bed and explained to me how her sons had lived here, how she had given them everything—designer jeans, Sega, a brand-new Ford Bronco—and gone to every baseball game. Their father never went. He was gone now, the older boys with him and the youngest daughter, too. She only saw the children on holidays, though never on Christmas.

"Marianne is the only one good enough to stay. She hates her stepmother. We both do. Alicia is her name. Pretty close to Alice, don't you think? I always thought that's why he married her, though I know it's only temporary. They don't even own a house. They have some kind of condo in the Cities, and the boys only went to live there because the baseball teams are better. Club teams, better colleges, you get the idea."

"And your daughter?"

"She was only three when Walter started leaving. He'd brainwashed her, told her I was a bad mother, bought her a million Barbie dolls and even one of those Barbie Jeeps. It was sick, what he did. But Marianne, she's a smart girl. She saw through it. She saw through his little girlfriend and the big allowance and promises of Mall of America every weekend. She's the only thing I've got."

"She's a nice friend."

"She's not his daughter—don't tell *her* that. I think he knows. That's probably why he said nothing when she wanted to live with me. So, in a sense, it was good what I did. Now Marianne is mine, and if it comes to a custody battle I can always have them check her DNA. Like on *The Maury Show*."

I felt my stomach lurch.

"Shit, I'm sorry." Mrs. Lorrey smiled at me through the gray dark. "There I go again, running my mouth. It's just, I felt you were someone I could talk to."

Wrong.

She walked along the edge of the room, tracing her finger around the baseball decals. "You've been through hell. You know how I feel," she said, picking at the corner of a Louisville Slugger. "I used to know your mom, pretty well, actually."

"You did?"

"From Fairest of the Fair. She was younger. She always won. Three times I was runner-up." Mrs. Lorrey went on about her life in Savannah, where she'd been crowned Little Miss Southern and Miss Georgia Peach. "It was hard moving here. I was only fourteen. I had never lost before."

She pulled the Slugger decal straight off the wall. "And now look at me."

I was looking, and I wondered how much longer this would go on, for me and for her. Mrs. Lorrey was a woman with an empty Victorian visited more often by tourists than by her own kids, a woman with photo albums full of beauty pageants back in Georgia, of thirteen-year-old Alice Lorrey beneath a spotlight, posing with a ukulele, in a grass skirt and coconut bra, getting crowned among a group of less beautiful girls, all losers, lined up and smiling as young Alice cried and bowed and touched her head, making sure the tiara was still there. There were pictures of four babies in bathtubs; of Marianne, bruise-kneed, climbing the elm tree in their front yard; of Mrs. Lorrey in that same velvet dress ten years ago.

We sat side by side, flipping through pages.

There was a goofy-looking husband with sun-bleached hair and a good tan, wearing holiday-themed ties. *When did he become bad?* I wanted to ask, looking at Mr. Lorrey in an Easter egg tie, holding Marianne in one arm and her sister in the other, a big red poodle at their heels. I pictured him now with Alicia-not-Alice. How long would Mrs. Lorrey wait for him to come back? How many nights would she spend in her lost children's bedrooms?

"Marty, we're both sad." She reached for another photo album. "I could tell when I first saw you in the Peter Rabbit play, fourth grade. Marianne, I was so proud of her, she was the rabbit. They had me make the bunny ears and cotton tail, but you, you were in the back, a little sparrow tucked at the end of the chorus line, holding song cards."

I remembered the Elmer's glue the boys had spread on my bare arms and the brown feathers they'd stuck on when Mrs. Matthews wasn't looking. There wasn't time to wash them off. I could still feel the sharp, needling prick of the feathers. When I'd finally gone on stage with my song cards, the audience had cried out in laughter as the damp, cool carrot nose flopped down on my face.

"I knew you were Glory's daughter without being told. I could see it all over you. That sadness. I pitied you, Marty, I really did." She paused at a picture of herself as a girl, a black-and-white smile dressed in a decorated sash and a crisp

Brownies uniform. "If I had only known then what was coming for me."

"They'll come back," I told her, though I didn't believe it.

"They will," she said, a catch in her breath.

She closed the photo album, and I leaned my head against her shoulder. I could smell the cigarettes. Suddenly they were everywhere.

"They will," she repeated, stroking my hair. "You'll see, there's nothing in this world like a mother's love."

I buried my face in the plush of her robe.

"Marty?" Her voice was as gentle as her fingers running through my hair. I hoped she wouldn't make me leave, go back to the girls. I closed my eyes and waited.

"This was your mother's house. You knew that, right?"

I said nothing.

"She grew up here. In this room."

That was probably why I hated it so much. Why it felt so lonely.

"I worried about your dad being back here. The memories."

It suddenly felt even crueler, him dragging me here. Letting me walk in. Driving past it a million times. Listening to Marianne's bullshit show-and-tell.

"And Marty?" There was something else—it was weighing on her.

"Never mind," she said. "Never mind for now."

CHAPTER EIGHT

Sylvia

When Bo pushed into the diner, Sylvia glared at Lars. She made quick circles with her index finger, mouthing, "Go, go, go." Lars knocked back the rest of his beer. Winked at her on his way out. Of course, he knew she loved Bo. Sometimes, in bed, they talked about him. "You wanna say his name?" Lars asked her once, in earnest. "I don't mind at all."

"God, no."

"What is it about that guy?" Lars had asked, amused. "Even my mom has a crush on him."

His mom. Probably closer to Sylvia's age.

"She says he looks like a young Warren Beatty," he said.

More like Harrison Ford. "It's more than good looks."

"What? His personality?" Lars laughed. "He doesn't have one."

"You don't know him."

"I've seen him at the bar. He's *weird*."

"He's not weird." Sylvia felt foolish for defending him. "He's quiet."

"That's the thing." Lars stood up, pulled on his shirt. "He's not. He used to talk all the time to anyone who'd listen. He was always cracking jokes."

"He was probably drunk. He's sober now."

Lars gave her a strange look. "He's *different*. To be honest, it creeps me out." He buttoned his jeans. "It doesn't matter that his wife left. That he was drunk then, sober now. Allegedly." He emphasized the word. "Your personality isn't supposed to pull a 180."

"You sound jealous." But he didn't look jealous. More like he was annoyed.

"Couldn't be." That was a slight on her. "Anyway, it's none of my business."

"The bar is low here. You know that, right?" *If looks could kill.* "We don't have a whole lot to choose from." Men had a habit of leaving; you couldn't swing your arms at the bar without hitting a single woman. It was like New York City that way, a numbers game. Twenty single women for every man, which meant guys like Lars and Bo could have anyone they wanted. The only thing weird about Bo was that he didn't seem to want anyone.

Hung up on Glory. But if he loved her so much, why didn't he stop her from leaving? Why wouldn't he say her name? Acknowledge, even in the tiniest way, that she'd ever existed?

"Let's not get nasty with each other," Lars had said. "You know I care about you *in a way.*" How nice. "I'm just saying, *Be careful.*"

Bo tapped the snow off his boots and sat down at the horseshoe counter. "You still seeing Larry?" he asked.

"Lars." Sylvia tried not to blush. "And no. Never was."

Sylvia had tried to keep Lars a secret. Impossible in a town like this.

Still, Bo was detached. He didn't gossip. He only had a few friends: another hunter on the island, that guy at the hardware store in Laurel, a workhand at the apple orchard who might've been his cousin. He didn't have a routine in town: he didn't meander from the bank to the post office to the diner like her regulars did. He had seemed normal in high school, socializing, playing football as his silent Scandinavian parents watched from the stands. They were farmers—good people but not good enough for Glory; as soon as she came into the picture, he had wanted to get away from them. The farthest he got

60 **Gichigami**

was the island, and he remained there, keeping the world at a distance. Sylvia only saw him on rare occasions—Marty's birthday and those times when she would *accidentally* run into him.

"You know me, single as ever," Sylvia added.

What she would've given for him to look happy, even slightly pleased, at her response. But Bo was blank-faced, like a person who asks a question to be polite but isn't polite enough to listen. "Someday, someday," he said.

"And you?" She tried to level out her voice. "You seeing anyone? You can tell me. I actually can keep a secret, despite what your daughter says."

He laughed, embarrassed. "Me? God, no. But I might have to take Mrs. Lorrey out if she keeps giving me jobs around her house. At this point, I think she's making things up, like replacing a green granite countertop with a beige one. Or having me push her couch around the living room until she finds the right angle, which was—you guessed it—back where we started."

His smile made her stomach ache. Sylvia felt the familiar pangs of jealousy. She had first felt that anger and envy, weighted with humiliation, when Glory was chosen over her to help their second-grade teacher, Mr. Carmichael, after class—with Lord knows what, now that Sylvia was thinking about it. Glory was front and center at every dance recital. The recipient of every passed note, Sylvia the messenger. As Glory grew more and more lovely, Sylvia suffered from acne, frizzy hair made worse with a perm, and a full figure that had gone out of style with the advent of the supermodel. Meanwhile, there was Glory: thin as a rail, commanding the room like Naomi Campbell.

"You like him," Glory had said to her once, both amused and sour. "You want him, you can have him. After everything he's done." They'd been right here in the diner, and Glory had plopped Marty into Sylvia's arms as if to say, *All this can be yours.*

Sylvia balled her hands into fists, pressing her red oval nails into her palms, and walked away from the counter.

"Alice Lorrey." She flung the coffee filter into the trash. "She's older than us, isn't she? Alcoholic. Divorced. But she's pretty, right? And she's got money, though I hear it's a lot less than she lets on." She wanted to look at him directly, gauge his reaction. But her expression—clenched jaw, forced smile—would betray everything. Her pathetic, ridiculous, unrequited love. Maybe it didn't matter. Maybe he'd known for years.

"I've got to tell you something about Mrs. Lorrey. It's bad."

"Bad?" Sylvia's voice peaked. "How bad?"

"I left Marty with Mrs. Lorrey, with her *and* the girls."

He told Sylvia everything: about the renovating job, the birthday party; how Mrs. Lorrey had paraded around the driveway and pushed her head inside the truck.

"I wanted to punish her, but this—you should've seen her face—this was mean."

Sylvia grabbed her purse. "I'll go. Grab her now."

"It's a sleepover."

She yanked on her coat. "You know what goes on at sleepovers? What girls do?"

"Hair stuff, makeup."

"They smoke weed. They get drunk. They torture girls like her."

As a child, Sylvia had adored sleepovers. There were only nine girls in her class so, for each birthday, everyone was invited. There were party games, ice skating, bowling, movie nights. Hot dishes and trick candles and secrets told under the dining table. In junior high, things got ugly. Only certain girls were invited (always Glory, never Sylvia), and when the parties rolled around, Glory would drag Sylvia along anyway. "Don't be a chicken," Glory would say. "They won't mind. They probably just forgot to tell you." It was worse, Sylvia thought, to be forgotten rather than disliked. To be disliked meant that somebody had, at the very least, remembered you.

When Sylvia did show up at these parties, uninvited, the other girls would say nothing to each other. There was not even an eye roll or a shared smile. They went on with the night as if nothing had happened. "See," Glory would say, nudging Sylvia. "I was right, wasn't I?"

After everyone had binged on frozen pizzas, laughed, truth-or-dared, smoked, and fallen asleep, Sylvia would lie in her sleeping bag, positioned slightly away from the other girls, glaring up at the ceiling. The thought of Marty glaring at the Lorreys' ceiling made Sylvia sick with grief. She wiped the sweat from her upper lip and called into the kitchen, "Back in ten."

Bo grabbed her arm. "Sylvia, don't."

"It's fine. It will only take a minute."

"That'll make things worse."

"They couldn't be worse. Those girls. *That* house."

"They'll tease her for leaving."

"What do you know about girls?" Sylvia tried pulling away from him, but he held her arm more tightly. "Let me go."

"You have to understand."

"You're hurting me."

"Marty can't leave her own birthday party. Think of Mrs. Lorrey."

"I don't give a shit about her." Sylvia tried to slip out of her coat and away from him.

Bo grabbed her other arm and pinned them together. She had never seen him look so mean. Her mouth gaped, and her arms went limp.

"Shit, I'm sorry," Bo mumbled, quickly dropping her arms. "But I need this, Sylvia. I can't lose the work."

CHAPTER NINE

Marta

In class on Monday, Marianne slipped into Rachel's desk, which was right behind mine, and whispered a million questions in my ear. What had happened? Why hadn't I slept in the tent? Why had I so rudely snagged her arm in the zipper? She showed me the scratch. How could I have missed her mother's famous French toast breakfast? She had even made a quiche, whatever that was.

When Mr. Purdy turned to face his diagram of the reproductive system, I leaned back toward Marianne and whispered, "I was sick."

"From the cigarettes?"

"From the cupcakes. Too much frosting."

Marianne shook her head. "I told my mom. I told her she went overboard." A second later: "You going to the homecoming dance?"

"No."

She passed a paper note folded up in the shape of a fortuneteller. Tried to force it on my thumb and fingers. "You'd better consult it first. Say a number," she said.

For the past few weeks, this had been how Marianne and Chelsea would answer any question or decide anything about any boy. They didn't hesitate to interrupt Mr. Purdy with laughs and screams when the fortuneteller revealed its answer. (They claimed it was 94 percent accurate, though they would need to live longer to test most results.)

I drew a sad face on my science homework, along with a dumb excuse that seemed to work for her: *Busy. Babysitting Sylvia's cat.*

Obviously, I had nothing to do. I would be alone that night. Dad was going to Sylvia's apartment to "fix a leaky sink," a line that sounded more made up than mine.

I hadn't talked to Sylvia in weeks. I was still mad about the dress. Even madder about her crawling nails beneath the glass table. Like all the mainland women, she had been waiting for her chance to catch Dad, and now she was doing it. All of those nights, while I was out searching for Mom, Sylvia had been stepping in. She had probably sneaked over to the castle, tried on Mom's leftover jewelry, and touched her side of the bed. Maybe she had even slept there. Been sleeping there for months. Was it Sylvia's voice in the dark, her high heels drawing me up from sleep?

She was clever, trying to get to me to get to Dad, asking me about boys, throwing me parties, buying me stupid gifts. I wondered how many times she had thought of stealing him when Mom was still around, when they were just teenagers. Now there was nothing standing in her way. Mom was gone, gone, just like Mr. Lorrey and the other children, who had left for some reason but mostly because they could. Because life was always better someplace else.

The week crept by. I avoided Marianne in class, and on Saturday I stayed in my room. Eventually, when the sun set and the whole world turned the palest blue, Dad came up to my bedroom. He stood in the doorway, holding a supper plate. A slab of gray meatloaf, a thick layer of ketchup. I was lying on the floor, reading my algebra textbook.

"You sure you don't want to come?" he asked. "Sylvia's been asking about you."

I slid farther from the door, so that my body was half-hidden under my bed and the dangling eyelet bed skirt.

Dad set the plate of meatloaf on my nightstand and stood there awkwardly.

I nudged my textbook with the tip of my elbow. "I'm busy, okay?"

"You haven't eaten all day. In fact, you barely eat anything at all."

Not that he ever cooked. "I'm fine."

"You don't talk to anyone."

I slid all the way under my bed. "I don't have anyone to talk to."

"Marty." He crouched down but didn't lift the bed skirt between us. "You can talk to me. I know you're sad about Mom."

"I don't care if she's dead."

It would be easier that way. Death parting us instead of a stupid choice she'd made. Then I could pluck all the black-eyed Susans that grow around the dump. Bring them to Mom's grave. Sit on the grass right over her body. Polish her gravestone with my beach towel. Scare squirrels away. Read her something from English class, maybe a bad poem I'd written. She wouldn't mind and, if she did, she couldn't say.

Dad lay down on the floor. He was sweating through his thick red-checkered flannel, a ring under each arm. He said, "Jesus, I'm sorry. I know how much you wanted to find her. The first few years, I felt that way all the time. I looked for her everywhere, in the woods, on the ferry, between aisles at the supermarket. I was crazy. Remember how I kept the porch lights on, doors unlocked? I was so sure she would stumble home one night and curl up beside me, knowing she was welcomed back no matter where she'd gone or what she'd done. It didn't matter. I just wanted to hear her voice again, even if she was saying something mean, like she'd never liked this house, never liked the island, that I was nobody, nothing. I wouldn't care, wouldn't fight. I would hold her so tightly she couldn't turn around and leave again. But she didn't come back. And I never got a chance to make her happy. You remember the way she laughed, how she'd keep going until she cried? I just need to hear it." He covered his face and swallowed. "But that's not going to happen. She's not coming back *again*." His voice snagged on the word.

"Again?"

"Not again." He curled his fingers into fists. "What I meant was ever. She's not ever coming back."

"You don't know that."

"I know," he said so roughly and with such conviction it almost destroyed me.

She wasn't coming back. I knew that. I'd spent all day, all week, feeling the weight of it. What I couldn't understand was why Dad wanted to throw it in my face. Confirm the most awful thing in the world and drag me through his pain, as if mine weren't enough. I could feel how much she'd hurt him. The rejection in his voice. Humiliation. I was humiliated, too, for ever looking for Mom. For thinking she would come back to us, pathetic as we were.

"I'm sorry about Mom and the birthday party and the dance. I didn't even know it was tonight. Mrs. Lorrey called to check on you. She wanted to know why you weren't going. Guess they're having another big party at their house." He was speaking so quietly I could barely hear him. "You want to go? I'll drive you. You can wear your overalls. You can have a beer. Whatever you want."

I shook my head, dragging a dust bunny.

"Two beers." He was trying to make a joke, but I gave him nothing. "You want me to stay?"

I wanted to say, *Yes. I'll be nice if you stay. Please, don't leave me alone.*

I tried to open my mouth to form the words, but my throat seized up. I breathed into my hands until my heart slowed, until I knew I wouldn't cry in front of him. We lay still like that, me under the bed and Dad on the floor beside me for ten minutes maybe. It was the longest he'd ever been near me, close like that.

"You want me to stay?" he repeated, easing up from the floor. "I'll call Sylvia. Tell her I can't fix her sink till tomorrow. Only—"

"What?" I pushed out from underneath the bed. "Only you really want to go?"

He plucked the dust from my hair. "No, but I should go."

"And leave me?"

"For an hour, maybe two."

"Because you like her?"

"Because I owe her. She's helped with a few things."

"So you won't stay?"

"Just come with. She misses you."

"Does not."

"What about the dance? I could swing you by for an hour. A half-hour."

"Leave already."

"I'll stay. Of course, I'll stay with you."

"Never mind."

"But Marty—"

"Go."

When Dad finally left, I sat cross-legged on my bed, the chilled plate of meatloaf and instant mashed potatoes in my lap. I prodded the slab of meat, tried to take a bite, but decided it was better to just smash everything together and eat it that way, without really knowing what was what. As my room grew dark, I finished the whole plate and went back to my textbook. My homework was already done, so I did practice problems and compared answers in the back.

I threw myself across my bed and imagined all of the minivans pulling up to the school to drop off my classmates in their better-than-church clothes. I thought of Mrs. Lorrey, all dolled up like the girls. She was saying, "Goodbye, have fun, take lots of pictures," while Marianne was rolling her eyes and making jokes about her mother's updo. All the girls were laughing into their hands and stepping out of the car, careful to avoid snowdrifts in their delicate Mall of America high heels. Mrs. Lorrey would be waiting curbside in the high school's parking lot, watching until the girls disappeared into the gym. She might wait even longer, watching other girls, other couples rush in before finally driving back to her empty house, where she would wait for a swift return, like I was waiting now.

Like magic, there was knocking. Slow and steady. I flicked off my bedroom light and slipped from the hallway into Dad's room, searching for his hidden safety rifle. It wasn't there. Neither was his baseball bat, so I rummaged through his bathroom drawers until I found an old can of hairspray. Whirling the can back and forth, I crept through the halls and down the creaky staircase to the bottom floor.

I stood behind the coatrack.

There was rough slamming, the sound of an open palm against the door, stopping once, then again, to twist the locked doorknob.

Maybe it was Mom. Maybe she thought I wouldn't answer the door if I heard her voice.

"Marta," someone shouted. "Open up. I'll throw rocks again."

Levi. I dropped the can of hairspray.

"I can hear you. I saw your bedroom light," he said.

I thought about sprinting back upstairs, but I knew he wouldn't leave. I ran my fingers through my hair to make sure the dust bunnies were gone, and then I opened the door.

Levi was standing there in a pressed white-collared shirt and a sky-pink tie. He had his long hair slicked back, a white lily in one hand. His sneakers, covered in snow.

"Your corsage," he said. "You know, you made me look like a real fool showing up without a date. Marianne said you'd be at Sylvia's watching her cat, but I checked. You weren't there. Your dad told me to come over."

"He told you to come here?"

"I'm good with parents."

"Liar."

"Me?" he said with a smile. "Sylvia doesn't own a cat."

He took my hand and slipped the corsage onto my wrist. It was small, but the whole thing felt like a rock tied to my arm.

"How long do I have to keep this on?"

"Looks good with the overalls." He stepped past me through the half-opened door. "If you don't mind, I'd like to warm up with a hot bev. Hot chocolate maybe? The walk feels much longer when it's ten degrees."

"Ten degrees is actually pretty warm." I crossed my arms, tucking the corsage into the crook of my elbow like an ostrich burying its head. "I walk the road when it's twenty below."

"Please. I've seen you wear a sweatshirt in August."

"Have not."

"Goosebumps when Purdy cranks the AC."

I laughed because it was true. We'd never had AC. I couldn't stand it. "You don't even have Purdy. How do you know that?"

"I know you." He smiled, and I felt hot all at once.

The only light in the kitchen was the tiny dying bulb above the stove. In the flickering darkness, I watched Levi heat the kettle. My mother was the last person who'd touched it.

A few pieces of his gelled hair teased loose from the steam. He poured two mugs of water, only spilling once, and tore open four packets of Swiss Miss, ancient and rocky. He had to work to get the contents out. We sat on opposite sides of Dad's oak table; between us, a rectangular slice of moonlight.

"Did you really see my dad?" I asked, sipping gingerly, immediately burning my tongue.

"Yeah, under the sink. I got really close to his face."

"Did he have his tools?"

"He was banging around down there."

"How did the sink look?"

"White bowl, pink flowers. Pretty standard."

"Did it look broken? I mean, really broken?"

"The pipe was mangled." Levi leaned forward. "Why you so interested?"

"Doesn't matter."

"You think he's lying?"

"What was Sylvia doing?"

"She was in the kitchen heating up SpaghettiOs. She offered me some, which was nice."

I scoffed. "What did she look like?"

"Uh, I don't know. Red hair. Like Sylvia."

"I mean how was she dressed."

"Oh, oh." Levi pulled at his tie, his fingers running against the slippery fabric. "Pajamas."

"Silky ones?"

"Let me think. Do you have a sketchbook?" He smiled.

"You were just there. Silk or lace?"

He dropped his tie. "Cat pattern. Funny how she's got cat everything but no cat."

"Hair done?"

"I remember a banana clip."

Sylvia was good, dressing down in case I happened to come over.

"Do you think they know something about your mom?" Levi pushed back from his chair and moved to the one closest to me. "Maybe they have an address. Did you ask?"

"No."

"Let's go over there. Ambush them."

"I'm not looking for her anymore."

His lips moved, a question hanging in the space between us.

We sat together for a long time, Levi sipping hot chocolate too hot to drink and me petting the smooth petals of my corsage. One big flower, its head like the mouth of a trumpet. I wanted to know why he had chosen a lily of all things—I had only ever seen these at funerals—and where in the world it had come from. The closest floral shop was hours away. I wanted to ask why he didn't stay at the dance with Marianne or run off to the afterparties. The VFW had the best hamburgers in town and was known for serving minors. There was the casino, too, which was hard to sneak into unless you knew somebody, which he did.

He knew everybody. Everybody liked him, which made it even weirder that he was here with me across the frozen lake in this house that was always freezing.

I pushed back from my chair. "Dance with me?" I asked.

His eyes met mine; they were skeptical. "Are you being mean?"

"I'm never mean."

"As soon as I stand up, you're gonna laugh like Nelson in *The Simpsons*."

"I've never seen that show."

When I stood up, he knew I was serious.

He pushed out from the table, rushing to clear a space between the table and the kitchen island. He swept away stray gloves, socks, and tools and pushed the recycling boxes into the corner. I put my hands on his shoulders. He drew his arms through the straps of my overalls and around my waist. We swayed side to side, making a slow turn in the kitchen.

"You want to put a tape on?" His hands were clammy on my shoulders. "Velvet Underground? Pixies?"

"Shh."

"I've got Cher, too. I know how you like her wigs."

I rolled my eyes.

The stove light flicked on and off, a quiet pattern. We made tight circles around each other, rotating more slowly each time. I pressed my forehead against his collarbone and smelled the starch of a hot iron. I didn't think of Mom. I only felt the warmth of his skin.

Levi rested his chin on the crown of my head, and I closed my eyes.

He worked his hand beneath my shirt and pressed his fingers softly against my spine. Gently, timidly, he tilted his chin until the sharp line of his cheekbone kissed my temple. Our lips were close, nearly touching.

"Marty," Dad called. He was standing outside the kitchen window, his face bone-white from the moon. "Lights on. Now." He tapped the glass and disappeared around the house.

There was time, seconds between the window and the front door. I leaned forward. Just as Dad yanked open the screen door, I kissed Levi on the corner of his mouth.

CHAPTER TEN

Sylvia

After Bo left, Sylvia sat in the dark on the couch, staring at the black television screen. She spread her hands over the spot where Bo had just been sitting. Warm, lukewarm, cold as the room. She changed from her hideous cat pajamas (a mistake, she knew) into a burgundy slip, stained at the waist with dots of olive oil, fingerprints in a line across her ribs. She called Lars and left a long meandering voicemail. She had meant to ask him over but ended up talking about Bo, how she had broken a pipe with a meat tenderizer, how he'd come over to fix it but couldn't, and how he'd stayed to watch TV but scooted away from her on the couch. "He couldn't get farther away if he tried. I threw myself at him. No, lunged," she said, boiling with disgust.

She hung up, writhing in self-loathing, and finally managed to get herself off the couch. In the kitchen, she leaned against the stove and spooned herself a few SpaghettiOs from the pan. Why had she made them for Bo? Why not something brilliant like fried whitefish and twice-baked potatoes or decadent chicken cordon bleu? Another mistake. Sylvia soaked the pan, scrubbed the dried SpaghettiOs from the sides, and snapped on her rubber gloves. Cleaning was the only thing that could remove him and everything else from her mind. She scrubbed the countertops, ran vinegar through the coffee pot, pulled all the condiments from the refrigerator and wiped clean the shelves. In the middle of rearranging the Tupperware, there was a knock on the door. Sylvia glanced at the clock. Just shy of 2 a.m.

She slouched against the cabinets. "Lars?" she called.

"Thought you didn't see him." The voice was muffled, but she knew it was Bo. Back here, at this time of night. Sylvia pulled herself up from the floor, straightened her slip, wincing at the oil stains. She checked her reflection in the microwave before opening the front door.

Bo's face was bright with cold, his stocking cap littered with snow. He pulled his hands from his pockets and rubbed them together.

"They were dancing." He let out a big galloping laugh and kept laughing until there were tears in his eyes. He couldn't catch his breath.

"Marty?" Sylvia asked. "And Levi?"

He managed to nod.

"And you're not mad?"

"Hell. I should be, shouldn't I?"

"So you're all talk."

"Ah, I can't help it. If you saw it, you'd be laughing, too. The two of them in the kitchen, shy and stiff-armed. Terrified when they saw me coming home."

Sylvia tried to imagine Marty dancing, her hands around that silly boy's slender neck. She was only thirteen but probably more loved than Sylvia had ever been.

"They still together?" Sylvia asked.

"I sent him home. Sent Marty to bed."

"And you came back here?"

Bo shrugged. He pulled off his stocking cap and his coat, careful not to let the snow drip on the carpet.

Sylvia laid his cap on the stove and flipped on the oven. He followed her into the kitchen.

"Not in any hurry," he said.

She looked at him, trying to understand what he was doing here, what he wanted.

She flipped off the oven.

Bo reached out and touched her waist, his fingers cold against the slip. He looked stranger than before, distant and smiling. If he hadn't been sober, she would've thought he was drunk. She took his other hand, guided it to her waist, and leaned into him. He smelled like rain and the flowery musk of the cabinet below her bathroom sink. She would've liked to remember the two of them dancing, shy and stiff-armed. But they didn't move.

She tried to crane her neck to kiss him, but he held her firmly to his chest. He placed his hand on her head and stroked her hair. This was the way he used to hold Glory, one arm slung around her waist and the other cradling her head, fingers deep in her pretty yellow hair. Sylvia remembered watching them at their wedding reception in the basement of the chapel. Their first dance. Bo was serious, completely still, as Glory twisted away from him, lips pursed, eyes searching for the camera.

Bo put his hand on the back of Sylvia's head, like palming a basketball, and pressed her face into his chest. Lips against flannel. She could feel his heart thumping, more and more quickly. Oh, God, was it finally happening?

She'd been waiting years for him to make a move, to give the slightest indication that he cared for her. This reciprocation, as small and innocent as it seemed, was everything to Sylvia. Love returned for the first time. A future with him and Marty, maybe more children. She was so happy she almost didn't realize he was pressing too firmly now, her lips and nose smashed against his chest. She couldn't breathe.

"Bo, stop." She struggled to pull away.

He squeezed her until the buttons of his flannel dug into her forehead.

"Cut it out." She shoved against him.

He quickly let go.

She staggered back against the counter. No, it wasn't happening. She didn't know what the hell was happening. A month ago, he had pinned her arms together to stop her from leaving the diner. And now he had tried to—what?—suffocate her?

As he knelt before her and took her hand and apologized,

red in the face, she could only hear Glory's words: "I can't tell you what's wrong with him, Sylvie, but it's *something*."

It had tortured Sylvia, seeing Glory and Bo together, witnessing the intensity of his love. Of course, she'd seen bruises on Glory's wrists; she knew he had developed a habit of following her, showing up wherever she said she was going to make sure she'd actually gone. He liked to listen in on her phone calls, check the withdrawals in their bank account. But was that really so strange? Didn't every man act like that when he really loved you?

In all these years, Sylvia had never taken it seriously that *something* was wrong with him. Now, for the first time, she wondered if Glory, who had always acted so tough, who had dismissed his behavior as "silly" or "annoying," was actually afraid of him.

Sylvia let her mind run wild, imagining fights that might've happened, that had led to bruises, stories that Glory had withheld. Maybe she had been trying to tell Sylvia in a million little ways that he was dangerous. Maybe she hadn't left to start a new life. She'd left to save her own.

But here was Bo, still kneeling on the floor, holding Sylvia's hand against his cheek.

"I'm sorry, please," he said.

Gentle Bo, who if guilty of anything, was guilty of loving someone too much. Sylvia knew exactly how that felt. She had long suspected, too, that love—real love—could change a person. That if she loved Bo, and Bo loved her back, things would be different. There would be no empty nights, no jealousy, no pain. Only tenderness between them.

"It's all right," she said, kneeling, wrapping her arms around him.

It was heaven when he hugged her back.

CHAPTER ELEVEN

Marta

The thaw came. Those were the weeks without Dad, without the drifting snow and the howling lake wind. The castle was quiet, a slow-building mess of dishes and clothes. The ferry was ferrying again. The ice was spreading across the lake, a broken mirror, melting in jagged slabs. Locals rode back and forth from the mainland to the island, clapping each time *the Island Queen* cut through a glittering sheet of ice, leaving thin, splintered bones in the ferry's wake.

I spent most days after school on the island's beach, dragging my heels against half-frozen sand and pulling abandoned kayaks, dinghies, and rotting swim noodles up the shore. The boats only needed a good scrub, a few patches. When summer came around, we would sell them back to the same tourists who had left them here.

Mrs. Lorrey didn't offer Dad another renovating job, though he had followed up about the granite countertop. Worse, she had paid him only a third of what she'd promised for the bedroom. Once, when we ran into her at Lucy's, she told Dad the rest would come when Mr. Lorrey returned from his business trip. "Paris is far away," she'd said, "and my husband doesn't have an American phone." She pretended to shop a little more and then abandoned her cart full of groceries. I felt embarrassed. Even though we needed the money, I told Dad to give her time.

In the spirit of the thaw, Sylvia bleached her hair, but it came out more copper than blonde. Onie thought she was trying to lift the redhead curse. I told her we both knew the real reason. She was trying to look like *someone else*.

Sylvia bought new clothes: tight denim skirts and a bunch

of low-cut tops. She carried little weights with her wherever she went and talked in a sweeter, higher pitch, as if she were possessed.

Whenever she was around, I didn't speak to her. And most days, I avoided her altogether. But once, after school, she followed me to the ferry and bought a ticket for herself. She sat on the bench in front of me, reading a wrinkled copy of *Vogue*.

"How's school going?" she said.

"I was thinking we could take a trip somewhere," Sylvia said. "What do you think of the Porkies? They got ski hills." Like she could ski.

"All done with the magazine," she said, holding it out. "Here."

She said, "We need to talk. There's something I need to tell you."

When the ferry finally reached the island, she stayed on her bench and hid behind her magazine. I didn't understand why she would follow me that far and turn back.

Dad was over at her apartment more and more, but she rarely came to the island. Maybe he thought he could hide what they were doing. But I knew. I wasn't so young. I couldn't sleep, thinking of them together in her bed. During those lawless hours between dark and dawn, I woke to every sound: the humming heater, the pelting rain coming hard against the roof, Dad's key shimmying into the front door.

Today at the beach, I found a flimsy rowboat beneath a pile of brush. No name: it couldn't belong to a local. With a little paint, the boat would sell for at least $40. Some tourist would marvel over the new coat, too distracted to notice the cracks in the hull. I dragged it from the beach, through the woods, to our marshy lawn.

Dad would've been proud of my $40 find, but he wasn't

home. The castle was dark and eerie, long, spidery icicles dripping down the siding. I yanked the rowboat forward and left it in front of the porch. Dad would have to see it there. If he didn't, if he were coming back late from Sylvia's, he would trip. Maybe whack his head and gain some sense.

At the front door, wedged between the door and the screen, there was a damp yellow envelope. The black ink was smeared, but I could make out the words. It was addressed to Dad. Blank return address. I tore at the corner of the seam and quickly sealed it up again. Dad was funny about mail; he opened everything in the shed and stacked bills under his toolbox.

I kept my boots on inside the house and marched up the stairs, leaving a trail of mud from the kitchen to my bedroom.

It was late when Dad came home. He said nothing about the rowboat. There was no hollering at the mud tracked in, no rattling of pots and pans in the kitchen. We wouldn't have any supper that night. Dad wouldn't even come upstairs. After a few hours, I slinked downstairs, my hand sliding soundlessly on the banister. I crossed the narrow hall to the kitchen and stopped short of the doorway.

Sylvia was at the table, her bleached hair pinned back in a banana clip, head down, one hand reaching across the table, inches from Dad's. His fingers were muddied from the ink, fingers curled around the yellow envelope. He kept his eyes closed. If I hadn't known them, I would have guessed they were praying. I wanted to scream at Sylvia and her stupid new hair. I wanted to push her from the room and make her disappear like Mom, but I couldn't speak. I stood in the hall, clinging to the doorway.

He hadn't replaced the bulb above the stove, so the room was dark. After a long stretch of silence, Dad crumpled the envelope until the paper shrank into a tiny ball.

Sylvia reached for Dad's hand. Slowly, painfully, he released the yellow envelope and laid his hand palm up on the table. Her fingers moved quickly, eagerly, interlocking with his.

I felt nauseous.

I ran back upstairs, to the cold cracked tile of my bathroom. Stretched out across the floor, staring up at the cobwebbed ceiling, I tried to think of anything but their hands, Sylvia's smile. It was late. I was too hungry to be hungry anymore and, eventually, after lying there long enough, I fell asleep.

In the morning, Dad was out front painting the rowboat. He must have been up for hours because the hull was already caulked and prepped for a new coat. Guess Dad didn't want the tourists to sink. I pushed through the front door, barefoot on the porch, and, for the first time since October, felt a little heat coming from the sun. I dipped my head back. In just a few months' time, the island would come alive again.

"No use trying to get a tan this time of year." Dad looked up from the rowboat, paintbrush in hand. "I could use some help." With a strained smile, he waved me over with the tip of his brush.

I stayed on the porch, my fingers pressed against the living-room window, smearing drops of rain until he went back to work.

"Is Sylvia still here? Is she in your room?" I pressed my finger hard against the window and dragged it across the surface, making an awful squeak.

He dipped his brush into the paint bucket. "She hasn't been by."

"You're lying."

He pulled the brush out slowly. "I'm not."

"Are too."

"It's none of your business anyway."

"I saw her."

Dad rolled out the hunch in his shoulders and looked up, the paintbrush slipping from his hands. It nicked his jeans and hit the ground.

"I saw you both," I said.

Before I could ask about the yellow envelope, Dad slumped down onto the muddy grass.

"I've got work to do," he said, running his fingers through the grass, smoothing the blades down flat. Out there on the lawn, he looked like an old man. I didn't want to fight with him anymore. I just wanted him to get up.

"I'll finish the boat," I told him, softening. "I can help."

"You can't."

———

That night, while Dad was back at Sylvia's, probably watching soaps and complimenting her new hair, I searched the kitchen for the yellow envelope. I pulled out thirteen different junk drawers, checking under spatulas and carving knifes, finding only random stuff: a bendable Goofy keychain, Roman candles and sparklers, Mom's poorly done crosswords, and a bunch of mini liquor bottles.

The trash cans had already been taken to the dump. Dad's room was empty.

He wasn't stupid. He had probably taken it from the house or was carrying it now. Maybe he had offered it to Sylvia, stashed it in her apartment. It was clear they were hiding something.

Under normal circumstances, I would've been fine sitting here alone. Scanning the TV for movies. *Twister. Labyrinth. The NeverEnding Story.* Eating Hungry-Man meals and whatever junk food was lurking in the back of cabinets. That's how it was when Mom left. A free-for-all.

Tonight, I was restless.

I wanted to call Levi. He was the only person I could trust, the only person I'd ever wanted to talk to. But when I picked up the phone to dial his number, the memory of us dancing made my skin crawl. That and my father's laugh as he'd come around the house to the kitchen.

The only other phone numbers I had memorized were

Sylvia's and the diner's. I flipped through my algebra textbook until I found a note scribbled in purple gel pen: Marianne's name in perfect cursive, a caricature of Mr. Purdy, and Marianne's phone number, smudged along the x-axis.

I hooked my finger around the seven rung of the dial and dragged my finger. I went for the seven again, then panicked, imagining another conversation with Mrs. Lorrey about her husband's Parisian trips, and released the dial. I went on like this for some time, playing cat and mouse with the phone until all seven of Marianne's numbers were dialed. Promptly, after the third ring, there was a small voice on the other end.

"Walter Lorrey's house." Her voice was higher pitched than Marianne's. She pronounced r's as w's, so the last name came out as "Lowwey."

"Who's this?"

"Who's this?" she repeated, mocking my surprise.

I dug my nails into the plastic telephone cord. "I asked first."

"Wainbow Lowwey."

"Wainbow?"

"Rainbow." She huffed against the phone.

"Your name is Rainbow?"

"Yes."

"Your mom is Alice?"

"Uh-huh."

"Is Marianne there?"

I could hear a scuffle on the other end, some scratching against the receiver, accidental dialing. Marianne said, "Chrissy, give me the phone." There was a struggle, a few mispronounced r's, a slamming sound as if the phone had been dropped.

Finally, Marianne recovered it. "Stupid Wainbow. She's been answering the phone all day like she actually lives here."

"Is she your little sister?"

Marianne paused. "Who is this?" she asked coldly.

"Marta."

"Oh, sorry, I thought you were my mom."

"Where is she? My dad hasn't heard from her in a while."

"She's been out."

"Where?"

"At my aunt's house. In Savannah."

"Where she used to do pageants?"

"Yeah."

"Is she doing more pageants?"

"Are you kidding me? She's old."

"Then what's she doing in Georgia?"

There was increasing silence between answers, and now there was no answer. We stayed together on the line, Marianne breathing softly, murmuring quiet admonitions to her sister. It went on like this forever, though in phone years it was probably less than thirty seconds.

"Do you want to come over?" I blurted out.

I could hear Rainbow's faint cries. She didn't want to be left alone.

"Anything to get away from her. What's your address? Do they have street signs on the island?"

I wanted to be annoyed, but half the roads were unmarked.

By the time I reached "Chebomnicon Road" in my address, I felt my soul leaving my body. What was I doing? She was coming here. She would see this house. My room.

She hung up.

I held the receiver between my shoulder and my head until I heard the bleating disconnected tone. I had heard this sound many times before, back when Mom used to call. It was only on scattered days, in those months after she'd left. The phone calls were never long. They were sweet but detached, like she was talking to a distant cousin.

"What's the snow like?" she would ask, knowing. "Have you pushed snow angels in the yard? Listen to your father. Won't you be a good girl?"

No, I wouldn't.

She would laugh.

"This is a pay phone," she would say, "and I'm running out of change. Say goodbye to him for me." I never did.

Then she would hang up, and I would stand there in the kitchen, listening to the bleat, bleat, bleat, my hands clutching the receiver, the cord wrapped around me like a snake.

Marianne showed up forty-five minutes later. None of the girls from class had ever seen the castle before. Most of them had rarely been to the island. If the mainlanders wanted to go anywhere, they headed to Laurel for the movie theater or Duluth for the mall, a two-hour drive. I'd never been there myself, but I'd heard Duluth was a huge city with mansions built into the hill overlooking our lake.

"I didn't know you guys had a beach," Marianne said.

I leaned against the front door, blocking the hole in the screen. "I mean, it *is* an island."

"Yeah, but like, I thought it was a bunch of rocks. Didn't someone die diving in?"

"Which one?"

Marianne made a face. "Is your dad around?"

"He won't be back for a while."

She looked relieved.

"Do you think he's weird or something?" I said.

"No." Her eyes told another story. "I brought something." She pulled out a pack of Virginia Slims. "My mom left these in her bathrobe."

"Won't she notice?"

She tapped a cigarette out. "She's not coming back."

We stayed outside. I built a tepee of dry wood in the fire pit, using Mom's old stack of *Glamour* magazines as kindling. Marianne sat cross-legged on a thick tree stump, counting the tree rings between her thighs as she smoked. "This tree was at least seventy-five," she said. "And then someone killed it."

The beauty magazines, now torn and buried under the stack of wood, quivered as they caught fire, the glossy paper rupturing in sour black smoke. A photo of Jennifer Love Hewitt walking two cocker spaniels writhed over the white coals.

The smoke was everywhere, drowning our clothes and hair in a smell that would take three washes to come out. With the wind pulling the fire in every direction, "White Rabbit" was a useless spell. The smoke whipped up at our faces; our eyes burned.

I sat on the grass beside the fire, and Marianne smoked the rest of the pack all the way through, a series of five cigarettes tucked between her fingers like a pouty magazine girl. In between drags, she told the story of her mother, though I hadn't dared to ask.

Walter Lorrey had come back from Paris (Texas) to a number of messages left on his answering machine in Saint Paul. Thirteen from Alice Lorrey, ranging from desperate to insane. She needed money. The mortgage was overdue. When was he coming back? Had he ditched Alicia? Not yet.

Mr. Lorrey had ignored the phone calls and had decided to withhold his contributions to her mortgage. So one night, Mrs. Lorrey showed up at his condo. When he wouldn't open the door, she threw a landscaping stone through a window—it happened to be Chrissy's. Thankfully, the window was on the other side of the room, far from Chrissy's bed. The broken glass only damaged a row of special-edition Beanie Babies. After a great deal of screaming and crying, Mrs. Lorrey left, running over Alicia's hand-painted mailbox on the way out.

Mr. Lorrey decided that his first wife was out of her mind and couldn't be trusted to raise Marianne. It was a miracle, he thought, that his daughter was still alive. He wouldn't be paying Mrs. Lorrey's bills anymore, and the house, well, it was in his name. The last thing he bought for Alice was a one-way ticket to Savannah, with two stops. Marianne would visit for Memorial Day or Mother's Day (her choice), Halloween, and next year's Easter, if Mrs. Lorrey behaved herself.

Marianne told the story like a news anchor would, with proper names for each family member and little interest in the outcome.

She said, "It's not so bad. My dad's never home, always back and forth to Texas. He does consultant work, whatever that means. And Alicia's not as bad as my mom makes her out to be. She takes me shopping, and she buys me the explicit version of whatever CD just came out. Plus, she used to let my brothers drink."

"So you like your stepmom?"

"Better than my mom—I mean, you've seen her."

"What's that supposed to mean?"

Marianne had this strange look on her face. "You of all people should understand what I'm talking about. She's *not well*."

I must've looked confused because she added, "She's an alcoholic. Like your dad."

I wasn't surprised that she knew, but it was shocking, hearing that word instead of something less incriminating like *drinking problem*.

"So what's going to happen to her?" I asked.

"Who cares?"

"And what about you?" The most popular girl in school moving away, leaving the kind of void my mother had left.

"You know, you're pretty nosy for a girl who doesn't talk."

"I talk."

"Mr. Purdy doesn't count. You haven't said a word in French. Chelsea has been watching you all semester. Aren't you gonna fail the class?"

"I hate French. And besides, I'm shy."

"You're not."

"Do the other girls think I'm weird?" I asked, trying to sound like I didn't care.

Marianne laughed, and smoke erupted from her lips.

"Do they?"

"You were pretty weird at your birthday. Tiff was pissed you left her scarf behind. Apparently, it took her dad three months to make that thing. Of course, my mom loves it. She wore it the whole week after you left."

"Do they hate me? You can say. It doesn't really matter."

Marianne pitched her cigarette into the fire. "We don't hate you. You've always hated us. You don't have to roll your eyes to actually roll them. It's that face you make."

"I don't hate you."

"You never talk to us."

"I'm talking to you right now."

"Only because you're sad." Marianne's words hung in the air like smoke.

"I'm not stupid," she finally said. "I know the way you look at me and Chelsea, the way you look at the whole class. You think you're better, which is hilarious. You're a year younger. I hear your mom was the same way."

"I'm not like her."

"She didn't have friends. Neither do you."

I pushed my fingers into the soft thawing earth. "I have friends."

"Who?" She was mean now, mean like she'd been to her mother.

"Levi."

"You're not a very good friend."

"How would you know?"

"Because he told me. Because I know him. We go to Al-Anon together. I bet you didn't know that."

I wasn't sure what that was.

"I bet you don't know anything about him," she said.

"He's my best friend."

"Oh, okay, so then you know about the Tennfjord boys, how they spray-painted a swastika on his garage door? You helped him paint over it?" She was gathering speed. "And you're well aware that his dad is dying? They've got a hospital bed in their living room."

I felt a sharp pain in my stomach. Levi had always seemed happy. I didn't know because I had never asked him.

"You know what was really sad?" she said.

I wanted to disappear.

"When you stood him up at the dance. He was standing there in the parking lot waiting for you. We were all waiting."

The fire crackled between us, and the wood ran down. She kept her head up, face turned toward the sky, her fingers tapping one by one against her knee, probably counting the hours until the first morning ferry at 6:07 a.m. Marianne was a nice person. It was clear now how much she hated me. How much I deserved it.

"Why'd you come here?" I asked.

Marianne stood up. She wadded up the empty pack of cigarettes and tossed it into the fire. "Why'd you invite me?"

My eyes ached. My jeans were wet and heavy, the chilly denim clinging to my legs. I wanted to go inside but couldn't because I knew she would follow me.

"Because of your mom," I said.

She kept her eyes on the half-moon.

"Because of my mom, too."

CHAPTER TWELVE

Marta

"If Jesus rose from the dead, you could at least wake up before ten." Dad's voice was loud and flat. He was standing in the doorway, blinking in the sun, dark circles under his eyes. "It's time for spring cleaning," he said, trying to muster some enthusiasm.

"I have a guest over."

"That Lorrey girl left on the ferry hours ago."

I felt immediately relieved but then horrified, remembering that I'd let her come in and had convinced her to sleep on the beaten-up couch with a musty blanket. (At least she hadn't seen my room.) I couldn't find an extra pillowcase, so I'd stuffed her pillow into one of Dad's nice t-shirts. She'd probably spent the whole night shivering, repulsed by everything and waiting for the ferry to rescue her. "Did she say anything about our house?"

"No, but I don't think she likes her new bedroom." He twisted a loose button on his sleeve. "What did you think?"

I shrugged, wanting him to suffer a little. "The canopy's pretty good."

He smiled, a real one. "Wish I'd gotten paid for it."

"You got some."

"Yeah, well we could use more. That's why I need your help."

Dad wanted to organize the whole house and throw a yard sale. We'd never had one before. Mom had always been embarrassed by them. She despised secondhand anything. Wouldn't even go near the fancy yard sales where you could find treadmills, skis, and electric pianos for less than $10, even cheaper if the day were nearing rain.

Ours wouldn't be one of those yard sales. All we had was

junk. "We're not going to make much money," I said. "And besides, I've got nothing to sell."

"Look around. Every dollar helps."

I surveyed my bedroom: flannels and jeans in a heap on the floor; sneakers, boots, and worn-down moccasins with missing beads; salt tracked from door to dresser; and, on the dresser, a stack of textbooks and the lipstick I had borrowed from the grocery store. "I'm not selling my stuff."

"I'm not asking you to sell all of it. Whatever you don't *need*."

On Easter, most families went to mass and pancake breakfasts and bought their children pretty baskets wrapped in iridescent cellophane. When Mom left, holidays did, too. And after Grandma Lotte and Grandpa Jan went, one after the other, Dad didn't feel the need to drive me all the way over to Saint Francis for Sunday mass. Some nights, I would press my palms together, trying to pray, but my prayers always came out as lists: everything I wanted for Christmas or for my birthday but never got, all the girls in class I didn't like and wished would move away (every girl—Marianne was right), all the mean things I'd said to Dad. I wanted to talk to Jesus (or to God, if it were more efficient) about Mom. I wanted to ask where she was, if she was ever coming back. I wanted to know why she'd left and, more than anything, why she hadn't brought me along. But whenever I thought about asking, I stopped myself. I was afraid God would answer.

I finally pulled myself out of bed at noon. Spring cleaning would take all night. The castle was taller than the trees and crowded with old boxes, all the things left in Mom's wake: half-smoked cigarettes perched on ash-marked windowsills, sponge rollers lost between cushions, stray Jujubes, her favorite candy, wedged like gemstones between the floorboards. The thought of throwing out her things made my stomach ache. If we swept up the cigarettes, we might lose her smell. Was Dad prepared to sell her vanity? Her winter clothes? Who would buy them in this town? No one, I tried to tell him.

He shook his head and sentenced me to the cellar.

I yanked on Dad's rubber boots and trudged through the yard to the cellar door. The lock was undone and hanging open on the latch; and during a moment of weakness, I thought Mom might be down there in her stupid pink coat. I wanted to close the lock and seal her in there forever so I'd never have to wonder where she was.

I ducked through the cellar door, pushing through cobwebs. At the bottom of the stairs, I flipped the lights on. There was water everywhere, more than a foot deep.

The cellar had flooded once before, but Dad had spent the whole day bailing it out with a mop bucket. A hundred trips up the stairs. He'd fished dead leaves from behind the stairwell and scrubbed the floors with a potato brush. He had always taken great pride in keeping an orderly house, but lately he'd been letting things slide. Dishes piling up. Salami molding in the fridge. Heaps of dirty clothes. He hadn't plowed the driveway once all winter.

Something was wrong. He was drinking again. Depressed, like he'd been the year Mom had left. Maybe that was the reason for the yard sale: ridding the house of Mom's things, every reminder. Or maybe he was falling in love, making room for Sylvia.

I didn't know much about love. I'd only ever seen it in the *Titanic* and *Pretty Woman*. I did know about liking someone, though. How I had felt, dumb and buoyant, after kissing Levi in the kitchen. Dad had never acted that way with Sylvia—at least, not in front of me. He wasn't happy or anything close to that. It was more like he was becoming less and less.

I waded through the icy water, stirring up a rotten smell. I ran my fingers along the shelves, grabbing cans of French-cut green beans, sweet corn, cherry jam, sliced potatoes, tuna. We could get a quarter apiece if we were lucky.

"Marty?" Dad called from the top of the stairs. "You doing okay?"

"There's water down here. And it stinks."

"That's why I told you to wear boots."

"So you knew about the water and you left it this way?"

"I've got bigger things to deal with."

"What things?"

He stared down at me like I should know the answer.

I spent another hour down there, gagging from the smell, and then went back upstairs with three buckets full of junk. The kitchen was a nightmare. Every cabinet and drawer had been flung open and emptied. On the counter were pots and pans, dishes, silverware, old crystal punch bowls, and Grandma Lotte's prized Prairie Gold china from her honeymoon voyage to Michigan. Everything was grouped into sections according to price, labeled with pink, blue, and yellow sale stickers.

I yanked a saucepan from the stack and hid it in the corner of the bottom cabinet. I grabbed forks, knives, and spoons and stashed them above the refrigerator, which had its own blue dot: "$25 or best." I scratched at the blue dot until it rolled beneath my fingernail.

How much money did we need? Dad was getting rid of everything.

"Dad, get down here." I slammed each drawer, waiting. I raced up the stairs, but he wasn't in his room, my room, or the guest rooms draped in tablecloths. There were price tags on my dresser, my alarm clock, all the gifts from Marianne's house, even the lipstick. I ran up to the attic. There were boxes of every shape, neatly stacked in the corner of the room.

The lookout was empty and, from the windows, I couldn't see him anywhere. But behind Dad's shed, I could see a huge burn pile. I ran down and stood beside it, feeling dwarfed and dumfounded. How long had it taken Dad to build this? Maybe weeks and weeks, hiding his work with a tarp. Maybe it had all happened this morning, before I had gotten out of bed.

The burn pile was taller than me, full of brush and a thousand crumpled pages: junk mail, letters, weather sections and funnies, pages torn from books, so much paper it looked like the mainland library had been ransacked. Everything wet and slimy, reeking of lighter fluid.

There were so many faces in the burn pile, more faces than I could recognize. Black-and-white photos of young boys jumping from sandstone cliffs; girls in cap-sleeve gowns with fur stoles, lined up next to a bride. She was beautiful. I pulled an album out of the stack and sent a flurry of paper flying through the air like snowflakes.

There were pictures of Dad with a bowl cut and freckles, playing hockey on the lake with his friends, their faces rosy; Dad in a tux waiting at the base of a staircase (Mom's old house); and, the best, Dad barefooting backward, grinning like a different person. There were pictures of Mom, too, posing on the ski boat, diving headfirst into the lake, glancing back as she pedaled her beach bike forward. There were only a few pictures of them together: one from the wedding, another camping on the island—Dad smiling, Mom pregnant and annoyed, holding a cigarette as far away from herself as she could, hoping it was off-camera.

I had never seen any of these pictures before.

I hid the album in the tool shed and went back to the pile. I dug my hands through the middle, grasping for more photo albums to save, but could only feel slippery magazines.

Lighter fluid was all over my hands now. They tingled, almost burned.

He had already tried to light the whole thing on fire. Near the bottom, the papers were charred, but the rest hadn't caught. Maybe Dad had run off to borrow the neighbor's truck so he could take it all to the dump. Get rid of everything before I noticed it was gone.

I kicked at the pile and sent the papers shimmying. There were huge torn up maps of Wisconsin, maps of Michigan's Porcupine Mountains, the fishing lakes of Ontario, and a pretty rumpled guide to Key West. There were postcards from Disney World, the Grand Ole Opry, and some island in the Caribbean. Some were made out to Dad, but most were addressed to me. The ink was blurry, the handwriting careless and fast: "Wish you were here," "You would love this sun," "Oh, how the other half lives!"

And there was her journal—a few feet from the pile, lying there in the dirt. He had taken it from my room.

The wind was picking up now, storm clouds gathering over the island. Rain was coming. It wouldn't be long. Maybe that was what Dad was relying on now, after he'd tried to light the burn pile but failed, failed to destroy this history of his life and Mom's life, too.

There was no way to look through everything before the storm came. I knelt in the needle-covered dirt and started tearing through the pile. There were dozens of pictures, so many faces staring back at me or flipped over in the wind to face the dirt, but there was no time to make out who they were or if they should be saved. I pushed record sleeves away from me. Tom Petty and the Heartbreakers, Sonny and Cher, the Cars, REO Speedwagon. All left to the storm.

I grabbed something that looked like tangled fishing line. It took me a second to realize it was yellow hair, tied with a ribbon. It had to be Mom's or maybe mine as a baby. Why would Dad have kept something like this? I dropped it, horrified.

The sky cracked.

I panicked. I thought about running for the door but couldn't bear to leave. The rain started slowly, breaking against the canopy first and then gently over my head.

The burn pile was everywhere, bits of newspaper rolling along the forest floor. I crawled deeper into the woods until my jeans were soaked in mud.

And there, lying on a trampled bed of moss, was a matted stack of letters made out in red pen, the cursive long, looping, and nearly impossible to read. I held the wet, translucent pages against my chest to shield them from the rain, peeking only at the first few lines of one of them:

Send something, anything. A school wallet? Won't you? I've got your pictures all over my vanity mirror, but I'm missing fourth grade.

March 19, 1992
Oh min kära,

It's been weeks, and it feels something like years. Are you a proper girl now? Have you learned to tap dance, sing, and shoot croquet with the ladies in town? Wear your hair in rollers? Drink tea with Librarian Loveless? I didn't think so.

I bet you're in your scruffy flannel PJs, tucked beside the fire with your hair undone, tangled down your back. Min kära, my little ragamuffin.

Yesterday you sounded so blue on the phone it almost broke my heart. I could barely bring myself to eat. Don't be sad, darling and, if you are, please don't say it's my fault. It was practically a hundred degrees in that stuffy telephone booth and another lady was tapping on the glass, waiting her turn. I had to go. And besides, I needed to save quarters for the laundromat. I so wish you were here to come with me. There are absolutely no entertaining people in Indiana, not one. I'm hoping Tennessee is livelier, what with Nashville and Dollywood.

You would die to see the Blue Ridge Mountains in the summertime. The air is warm and heavy but cool with the breeze, and the hilly blue stretches on for miles. It's ghostly when the night turns and the fog rolls over the valley. You were there once as a baby. It was a long way from your nana's new house in Nashville, but how we loved the drive. Your father let me choose the radio stations for sixteen hours straight! Sixteen!

Anyhow, I'm off. I know you don't miss me too much, but let's try to talk this week or next. In the meantime, be a help around the house, especially with the cooking. Your father's just learning suppers without me. Don't let him burn down the house! And be nice. I know that's hard for you!

—Love always, xoxo

August 12, 1992

Min kära,

I've sent at least six letters and left a dozen messages, but you've said nothing back. Have you been busy camping on the islands? Too busy to answer the phone? The distance between us has been hard on you but cruel to me. I am your mother whether I'm with you or not.

Next week, I'll be staying at the Southern Belle in Florida. Please write back and tell me all about your summer break from school. I wish I were there with you, out on the porch, braiding your hair and rubbing sunscreen across the bridge of your nose. Be careful not to burn.

Tell Sylvia hello for me and ask her to teach you to skip rocks on the still evening lake. Once, she threw a stone all the way from the mainland to the island. Over a hundred skips! You don't believe me, but I swear she's that good. And when you're through with skipping, be sure to ask Onie to patch your winter clothes. She's easily annoyed but soft at heart. She'll likely do the mending for free. Do something nice in return.

Sorry to run out of paper now, but these motel notepads are so desperately small. Stay up past bedtime and watch the meteor shower tonight. I'll be watching, too, and it'll be just like that time we snuck out after dark and left your father snoring on the couch. Remember how the northern lights danced across the sky—the purple night with strokes of daisy yellow and prairie green? Tonight, I'll make a wish for you.

—xoxo

October 24, 1995
Marta,

Send something, anything. A school wallet? Won't you? I've got your pictures all over my vanity mirror, but I'm missing fourth grade.

I'm sorry for getting angry with you in my last few letters. You surely don't deserve that from me, but how many times should I have to apologize? Don't you ever want to take a long vacation? Don't you want to see the world? Meet a whole bunch of new people, maybe someone as special as you?

I've been so many places. The Blue Ridge Mountains. That famous smoky blue, just like I said. I've lain on Elvis's grave. Danced in the famous Jungle Room. I've stopped at souvenir shops and BBQ shacks on gravel roads. Let my hair soak up the smell of ribs and honey. I've touched the ocean. Swum down to the coral and listened to the humpback whales. They sing to each other, min kära. Can you believe it? From miles and miles away.

All of these places and all of these people. Strangers and friends. But, remember, not a moment goes by when I don't think of you. I wonder what you're doing now. Though it's past season and the water's turning cold as ice, I am picturing you now standing knee-deep in the sea caves, picking wild raspberries and staining your lips a bright sugary red. Be careful of the riptides. I wish I could dive down and sing this underwater, long and sweet and sad, so you'd hear me. So you'd listen, even if you didn't want to.

—xo

March 6, 1998

Marta,

You've made it quite clear that you don't want to hear from me, but today I cannot help myself. Twelve years ago, the snow was falling so softly outside my window, and I knew in my heart spring would be here soon. The air was icy, but the snow blanketed the yard in the purest warm-white when we drove from the island to the hospital in Laurel. This was the day you were born.

Tell me, is the snow falling now? Is there a pretty blizzard sweeping the lake?

Outside my window, the grass is dead, the muddied earth cracked from heat, but I have an orange tree in the backyard, and it's full of tiny white blossoms, sticky to the touch. The tropical wind pulls the blossoms free from the branches. They fall to the earth like snow, min kära, and suddenly I am at home. It isn't anything like the island, those cozy, snowcapped bungalows and our old house, but I have a place of my own. It's small and crowded with the kind of secondhand furniture I swore I'd never buy. The backyard is withered now, but when the rain comes back, the dead grass will grow again and the bougainvillea will bloom.

I wish I could send a bouquet for your birthday, but the flowers wouldn't survive the distance and, besides, you'd probably throw them out. You're angry, still angry. I don't blame you.

In another year, you won't be a child. You'll be a teenager, hopefully much better than me. Sylvia, too. We were always in trouble. Have you been to the marina bar? Please say no. Do you have a boyfriend? Has anyone kissed you?

Please tell me, do you ever dream of me, our summers in the garden, nights out on the cliffs? Do you remember the good stuff—wind in our hair, stars falling, watching storms roll in over that gleaming pink lake—or is it only bad now?

—your mother (remember?)

CHAPTER THIRTEEN

Marta

"We're losing the house." Dad stood in the doorway, his arms full of rain-soaked letters and postcards.

I curled up more tightly on my bed, letting my wet clothes drown the sheets beneath me.

"I know you're mad, Marty. You ought to be."

I slid my hands beneath my pillow. My nails ached. I had scratched off every sales dot in my room, in the whole house, before Dad finally came home.

"It was pouring," he said, "but I ran around the woods. Tried to save what was left."

I turned to the window. The sky was so dark you couldn't see anything, but I could hear thunder building in the distance, booming like those caves along Devil's Island.

"I'm sorry," Dad said. "I didn't want you to find out this way."

"You didn't want me to find out at all."

"About the house?"

"About Mom."

I heard Dad sigh, then a cascade of paper. He had opened his arms. I turned to stare with him at the lifeless pile, at the gruesome bleeding ink. There were pictures, smudged cursive notes, and yellow notices shredded from the storm.

I didn't understand it then, what Dad meant about the house. All I could think of was Mom and her letters, how Dad had hidden them and how Mom had blamed me for not writing back. So many times I had wanted to talk to her, ask questions about school, the other girls, the right clothes to wear so they would leave me alone. I needed to know how to cut my own hair, how to make dinner—something that wasn't frozen—and how to tell someone I liked them.

Now I needed to know how to live without my room, without our house.

My body was frozen, prickling with pain, like I'd fallen through the ice.

The rain was pelting my window; the sky flashed, and thunder shook the house. Everything Dad hadn't saved would be ruined. He stood there, his mouth hanging open. Nothing to say. Eventually, he crouched down, picking up each postcard, letter, and picture and laying it out flat against the floor. He left and came back with Mom's blow dryer. He sat on the floor, running the barrel back and forth, until each piece of mail was puckered but dry.

He'd been lying about the house and, worst of all, about Mom. I hated him, even more for what he was doing now, trying to save the letters he'd just tried to burn. He knelt in the dark and offered up a single postcard, edges burnt but the picture still clear: a dancing alligator.

"Read this one. You have to," he said.

"I don't have to."

"Please, Marty."

"Get away from me."

Dad winced. He lay the postcard on my nightstand, stepped carefully over the letters on the floor, and disappeared through the doorway. I could hear his footsteps, then the sound of his weight leaning against the wall. He was waiting in the hallway, trying to be quiet.

"Go farther," I called.

His footsteps were slow, gentle on the stairs. I closed my door and grabbed the postcard. "The Achy Alligator, Pompano Beach" was printed on the top left corner. The handwriting was Mom's cursive—rushed, dotted with coffee stains:

Keep her away from me, then, if you think it's best. I'm sorry for leaving. But please understand. From the very start, I was living someone else's life. Do you know how that feels, to live each day where you've never belonged? I had to go. ~~Wouldn't you have done the same?~~ Don't say. I know the answer. You're better than me. But wasn't there a time when I was good, too, way back when we were darlings, when we used to say min kära and mean it? Please, min kära, tell our daughter I was good once, even if it isn't true. —G

But it was true. Mom was good. She hadn't really wanted to leave. It was my father who had driven her to it.

I sat on the floor and paged through her journal. I couldn't tell who was writing what, whether the words were hers or Levi's mom's. No single passage felt familiar.

I read the letters and postcards next, hoping this would be a version of my mother I recognized. It was. They were sweet, full of nothing. Pretty images of the places she had traveled through, followed by "Please write back." She never included a return address. Only motel names: Candy's Blue Lagoon, Silver Sands Motel, Casa Paradiso, Star Lite.

It was incredible, really, how little she gave away. After reading everything there was, I still knew nothing about her. Sure, I had a good idea of where she'd been. I knew she'd felt bad, more for herself than for me. But I didn't know what her life had looked like. If she'd had a job. If she'd gotten married. If she'd had another daughter. A dog. If she had actually loved me or was more concerned, given my lack of response, that I didn't love *her*.

Among her letters, there were warnings from the bank—nice, sympathetic, and then angry as years flew by. Finally, near my nightstand, Dad had laid out the yellow letter. It was a foreclosure notice from Chelsea's father, the president of the mainland bank. The auction sale was scheduled for two weeks from now.

Dad had not asked Sylvia to move in with us. We were not throwing a yard sale to get a jump on spring cleaning, to make a few bucks. We were getting rid of everything that couldn't fit into a suitcase.

———————

I watched from the lookout as locals and early tourists came and went, with my dresser, my shoes, the stolen lipstick. Mom's vanity went, too, along with her costume jewelry. Her cherry-stained apron, along with the whole kitchen, went to Sweet Caroline Inn, a new B&B on the island. The owner was a tall woman with bright red hair like Sylvia's. Her daughter's hair was red, too. They had both frowned at the card tables, at our china. They didn't touch anything, only pointed as Dad loaded dishes and appliances into the back of their neat red car.

That night, Dad was sitting at the table, pulling wrinkled dollars from a Mason jar and making small piles of tens and twenties.

"You hungry? We've got cereal, those tiny boxes you like," he said.

"And milk?"

Dad paused. "We can go to the store. I'll let you pick out anything."

"You don't have the money."

He nudged the Mason jar. "We have a little."

I pushed the stack of tens from the table. "You built the lookout. Painted the whole house blue when you knew we were losing it. You knew we were broke."

Dad bent down and gathered up the bills. "We're not broke. When Iris picks up this table, we'll have another fifty bucks."

"And nothing else."

"What was I supposed to do?"

"Tell the truth."

"I told you I was behind on things. Why do you think I took Mrs. Lorrey's job?"

"These things don't happen overnight."

"I know, I know." He massaged his temples, working circles into his pale-green skin. He looked so much older now, hunched over in the chair, his five o'clock shadow coarse and silvery. Mom wouldn't even recognize him if she ever did come home. But, of course, she wouldn't come back now. There was nothing to come back to.

"Marty, I let you down."

"More than that."

"More than that," he repeated. "But try to understand. There's no work on the island. The bills kept coming. I should've said something—I know—but I didn't want you worrying about money. You had enough to worry about."

"What about Mom? You had to lie about the letters, too?"

"You don't get it. I had to keep her away from you. She was hurting you—I saw it in your eyes every time she called."

"You're the one who's hurting me. You're the reason I don't have a mother." I kicked the leg of his chair. "She left because of you."

He blinked at the ceiling.

"You stole her letters, tried to make her look bad," I said.

"She *was* bad."

"You kept her from me."

"To protect you."

"To punish her. And you didn't care that it killed me. Every birthday. Every time some stranger whispered her name and stared across the diner. Whenever I passed your room and she wasn't there, which was always, for seven years. You're the reason she's gone."

His eyes flicked down from the ceiling, and he looked right at me. Big eyes. Full of something but saying nothing.

"No mother. No place to live. Where we gonna go? A motel? A campground? Some shack in the woods?" I asked.

"I think you know."

"Not Sylvia's. You can't."

"We've got no place else."

"You can't make me."

"Please, Marty. Don't make me feel worse."

"I'll find Mom. I'll call the motels. Find a number, her address."

"You won't."

"I'll live with her. She wants me to."

"You'll never find her."

"I won't stop looking."

His voice was flat and cold. "You should."

———

That night, I didn't sleep. I tried to call Levi, but our phone had been disconnected. All I could do was lie in my room, pretending not to notice the empty spaces. I had a bed, a stack of textbooks, a couple of flannels, ripped jeans, and thick cable sweaters too itchy to wear. And my Doc Martens—I couldn't live without them. "If you need anything else," Dad had said, "you can borrow from Sylvia." We both knew I would never do that.

Without the mismatched chipped furniture, my room felt huge and lonesome. I could no longer hide among a crowd of things or stow myself quietly in the lookout. In two weeks, the castle would belong to someone else. Or, worse, they'd knock it down. I touched the paper snowflakes hanging in my window. Pressed my fingers into the ash stains on the windowsills. All night, I walked and walked through the house while Dad slept, still as a corpse.

I slipped into each of the spare bedrooms and felt their emptiness, too. The heating pipes hummed through the walls. The house creaked with every step and every storm. This was the heaving, uneven rhythm I would miss—the surging copper pipes, the patter of rain and snow on the roof, set against the island's heartbeat. The birds calling out, wind tearing through the trees, waves rolling in the distance.

CHAPTER FOURTEEN

Sylvia

Sylvia scrubbed her apartment with a toothbrush and a gallon of vinegar, willing her apartment to smell fresh and clean and unlike the den of a sad single woman. She picked up the latest Penney's catalogue and ordered flare jeans and cardigans and crisp white tennis shoes for Marty. The cost was more than she made in a week. She grabbed her purse and ransacked the aisles at Lucy's, grabbing everything she had ever seen Marty eat: macaroni and cheese, cheeseburger helper and ground chuck, instant mashed potatoes, canned corn (no green beans!), Coke, and pancake mix. She laid everything out on the kitchen counter, arranged like a still life.

She knew she was trying too hard. Marty would never feel at home here, especially after learning that Sylvia had lied to her. Well, she hadn't lied exactly. But she'd known Marty was losing everything. She'd seen the letters; she'd tried to make a payment to save the house. Bo had stalled, and then had pulled the rug out from under Marty's feet.

For hours, Sylvia stood at the open living-room window, wiping the sweat from her upper lip, waiting for them to come. Once, during this intermission, Lars called, and she told him to never call again.

CHAPTER FIFTEEN

Marta

The castle looked like an abandoned house, ruined over centuries. Every scratch in the floorboards Dad had tried to hide beneath chairs and rugs was now exposed. There were spreading watermarks on the ceiling, mold creeping in the attic, and cottony yellow insulation spilling from the walls. Before we left, I stood in the yard, gazing up at the ill-fitting add-ons, the leaning lookout and its fading swamp-blue paint. Now I saw what everyone else had always seen. A dump.

As we crossed over to the mainland, I ran to the back of the ferry and watched the island shrink. I wanted it to sink into the lake, our house along with it. Four stories zigzagging to the bottom like a feather falling. Landing on the sand beside the shipwrecked *Lucerne*, somehow fully restored. I would've given anything to stay there.

Sylvia's brassy blonde curls bounced as she took my suitcase and showed me to my cot in her television room, which was the same room as the dining room. Sylvia's apartment had been built above Mimi's on the main strip, two stores down from the diner. It was a tiny one-bedroom—all of it could fit into our living room—with a rickety fire-escape entrance and "vintage" furniture from Vinnies: burnt-orange sofas, matching drapes and shag rugs. Mustard floral wallpaper. Trinkets everywhere, cats among them. Frozen in a variety of poses, the whole place frozen in time. Her apartment was like a portal to another world, one that I wanted no part of.

When she was out on errands, I looked through her stuff. I found dog-eared books—

Wuthering Heights, Sex and the Single Girl, You Can Heal Your Life—and a bunch of receipts from the diner on which people had scribbled "thanks!" and "nice waitress" and "you were the best part of the meal." I found a couple of phone numbers, one ripped in half and taped back together. There were pictures of Mom crammed into drawers. But no blue dress. Not in her closet, not anywhere.

She was good at hiding things, better than Dad.

A week after moving into Sylvia's place, I still hadn't said much to her. Once I asked if she'd gotten any postcards from Mom. "No, but I would've loved to," she said. Another time, I asked her to pass the scalloped potatoes. She was so happy I'd spoken to her that she nearly dropped the bowl. Most nights she hovered near my cot, offering cat-embroidered pillows and crocheted blankets until I pretended to fall asleep. Dad spent his nights on an inflatable camping mat, or so he claimed, which sat in the corner of Sylvia's room, and he stayed out most days looking for work, as if a renovating job could bring back the house.

The whole town knew we were broke. Everybody was talking about it, running gossip about the yard sale, the auction, and Sylvia's crowded apartment. *Finally got what she wanted*, people said.

The first day back at school was the worst. While Marianne, Chelsea, and all the tallest boys in class took down Easter decorations, I sat at my desk waiting for Mr. Purdy to stop asking if I needed help with my world history quiz. He pulled his chair next to me and explained the beheading of Marie Antoinette and the "shameful but totally, totally understandable" violence of the starving peasants. I endured his long-winded explanation while the class, oblivious or pained by the situation, ignored us both.

Our family name appeared in the local newspaper, the notice for our public-record bankruptcy printed next to an ad for the estate auction on Chebomnicon Road. The island was prime real estate, people said, especially come summertime. How fast would my house go and for how much? Maybe it was so bad they'd have to pay someone to live there and clean it up.

Would the auctioneer speak about the growing mold like lady fern in the attic or the foot of stagnant water in the cellar? Would potential buyers laugh at the chipped swamp-blue paint or lean over the stony edge of the wishing well, where a few unlucky animals had fallen?

I glanced back at the Red Cliff kids, dozing, their sneakers kicked up on desks. Namid yawned, lifted her head sleepily, and smiled at me. Rachel passed me a note. It was from Levi. I tucked the note into my desk without opening it. I couldn't face him yet. His pity would be stronger, inescapable.

During lunch, Marianne tried to buy my tray. When I refused, she grabbed a hamburger for me, "just for fun." Connie, our lunch lady, watched from a distance. She winced when Marianne waved the hamburger in my face and eventually turned away altogether. When we got to the end of the line, she glared at Marianne but didn't meet my eyes when I handed her my reduced-price ticket.

Instead of eating at the rental dock where I used to meet Levi or down at the mossy picnic table where I used to sit alone, I followed Marianne to the table of ninth-grade girls. As they talked and talked about the new varsity soccer player, Joaquim, an exchange student from Brazil, I did all I could to forget who I was and join in. "What about the baseball short-stop?" I asked. Teddy Bainbridge was old news. But instead of laughing at me or rolling their eyes, they tried to be nice. Chelsea and Rachel took turns offering me their lip gloss. Tiff gave me her last piece of gum. I caved and ate the hamburger more slowly than I wanted to.

On my way back to class, I passed some girl standing at her locker, poised in front of her magnetic heart-shaped mirror, pushing her long black hair into a ponytail. She was older, a cousin of Levi's, and she was wearing my dress, the one Mrs. Lorrey had given me. My knees nearly gave when I realized what was around her neck: Mom's freshwater pearls. Somehow Mom had forgotten to take them when she left. They had always sat in a perfect loop in a glossy white box in the top drawer of her vanity. I hadn't been allowed to touch them. "These are special," Dad had said. "I gave them to your mother on our last anniversary." I'd figured he was keeping them for me, for when I was grown up and beautiful—not like Mom, but pretty in my own way.

As kids pushed past me, nudging me with careless elbows and backpacks, I stood, center-hall, trying to breathe slowly, evenly, my stack of textbooks sharp against my collarbone. I tried to imagine the families in Laurel crammed into trailers or defunct collapsing farmhouses—"the real poor," Dad would say—but I could only see this girl in my clothes, adjusting the wandering clasp of Mom's necklace. I had never wanted the dress, but I needed the necklace. And I couldn't ask for it, not in the hallway with everyone watching, not ever. It would be the most shameful thing in the world.

―――――――

When I got home from school, Dad was sitting at the kitchen table, not eating, not reading, no TV. Just staring down at his hands. "How was school?" he said, jumping up from the table.

I glared at him and then at the shag. The orange pile had all been swept neatly toward Sylvia's bedroom.

"I vacuumed," he said, as if I cared.

I shrugged off my oversized jacket and dropped my backpack on the floor. All of my things were rippled with rain. I watched as the heavy beads of water slipped down sleeves, collars, straps.

"We should try to keep things nice here," he said. "School okay?" He tried to smile.

I kicked off my muddy boots, one near the glass table, the other onto the kitchen linoleum.

"Marianne tried to buy my lunch. Everybody stared at me."

"Because you're the prettiest one." Dad stubbed his toe into the carpet. "Jealous, is all."

"Not jealous."

"Yes. Jealous."

"No," I said, mean as I could. "Sorry."

I waited. His face was red when he looked up at me.

"Some girl was wearing my dress." I brought my hand to my collarbone and felt for the empty space around my neck. "She was wearing Mom's—"

Dad went over to the sink and buried his hands in last night's dishes. I followed him into the kitchen and stood beside my dripping boot. "Everybody knows. They all saw," I said.

"Saw what?" Dad paused with a dinner plate between his hands.

"The paper."

He scrubbed at the plate, dumped it back into the sink, and went to work on a pie tin.

"I'll get the house back," he said softly. "You'll see."

"Don't lie."

He wrung out his sponge. "I'm doing the best I can."

I looked around the apartment. "This is the best you can do?"

Before he could answer—not that he would—I grabbed my boots, slipped them on, and ran out the door. I walked up and down the street, avoiding Jaybird's. I could see Sylvia behind the counter, chatting up her customers. She was probably gossiping about us, saying she and my dad would be getting married any day now.

Above me, the sky was turning pink, clouds big and heavy. There had been a break in the rain but a storm was coming, and I had nowhere to go. I could follow the street to the top of the mainland hill. I could walk to Laurel, but I couldn't get farther. Buses cost money, and I'd heard hitchhiking was dangerous. There were stories of women getting into trucks and disappearing or, worse, getting dumped in the woods. But if I were careful, maybe I could make it south, all the way down through Wisconsin, through slices of Illinois, Indiana, Kentucky, Tennessee, and into Florida, where the stupid sun shined each and every day. Where was this place with orange blossoms, where she lived on her own, still loved me, and wanted me to visit? She hadn't said that, word for word, but she missed me. She had said that much. And if I showed up at her door, she wouldn't have the heart to send me back. She would listen to all of the terrible things Dad and Sylvia had done. With a mother's knowing, she would already have my bedroom fixed up, better than Marianne's, with a huge canopy bed and shelves of souvenirs from everywhere she'd been during our time apart.

I rushed up the hill, past the spooky chapel and the grave-yard tucked behind it, to where the highway met the street like a T. As I started walking down 13, the wind picked up, then the rain. Already, I was freezing. I wanted to go back for a raincoat, another pair of socks, whatever money I could steal from Sylvia's apartment, but Dad would be there and, sometimes, in those rare moments when he really looked at me, he could tell what I was thinking.

The highway was narrow, without shoulders, terrifying where the pavement met the cliffs. Luckily, it was mostly empty, so I walked in the middle of the lane.

Eventually, the rain stopped and the clouds parted. I watched as the sun, pink from the storm, collapsed into the lake, as if it were as tired as me. My feet ached. I was getting blisters from the wet leather rubbing on my ankles. I gave myself a minute to rest. From way up here on the cliffs, I could see the looming shores of Laurel, its massive ore dock reaching out to sea like a road leading nowhere. That was exactly how this felt.

The highway bent away from the lake and, in this stretch, I could see abandoned farmhouses, big open fields with skeletal tractors, a few cars, a boat that someone was probably living in. There were small nocturnal creatures roaming these open fields, their eyes like fireflies glowing in the distance.

I had no way of telling how much time had passed or how many miles I had gone, only that my legs and arms were so numb that I couldn't tell if my jeans were still soaked or only cold. Why hadn't Dad come yet? Wasn't he looking for me? I imagined him on the couch with Sylvia, the two of them flipping through the TV guide. He probably hadn't noticed I was gone. Or *Good riddance*, he might say.

After so much nothing on the highway, I felt the ground begin to tremor. The fog was thick, but I could see a pair of headlights creeping toward me. I waved and waved my arms. Hitchhiking would be better than freezing out here. As the truck drew closer, the ground shook and I could make out massive tires, as tall as me, and a single face at the wheel. The truck slowed down. I could see the driver was smiling.

I panicked. I raced into the field and lay down in the switchgrass.

The truck came to a noisy stop. I could hear a car door, a voice that seemed kinder than his face had looked. "I can help you," he shouted. "Little girl." I waited a long time, until I heard him heave back into the truck and pull away. I sat up and watched the truck disappear into the fog.

Odds are, he was nice. Maybe he could've helped me. Maybe this was how Mom had found herself moving farther and farther away from us, passing time with strangers. Accepting rides and Happy Meals and truck-stop cinnamon rolls bigger and sweeter than the ones at the diner back home. Not that she would mention it. She had never felt at home here. She probably loved the anonymity, reinventing herself like a little actress. Letting the memory of us fade like a bad dream.

Clouds gathered, splintered, and spread out across the black sky. I lay there in the prairie, too tired to move. It was warmer here, the tall grass blocking the wind. I drifted in and out of sleep, waking suddenly to a quiver in my limbs, as if I were falling from the cliffs.

No cars passed, only quick footsteps. Out here, there could be foxes, skunks, opossums, coyotes, or wolves. They were hungry, some starving and mangy, but none were looking for me. Black bears usually kept to the woods or, occasionally, to a neighboring campground, where they would help themselves to chips, s'mores, hot dogs, whatever the tourists had left out. A few times they'd busted through screen doors, barging into kitchens where a pie was cooling. They never tried to maul you, not really.

The ground began to vibrate. A pair of lights cut softly through the fog. In the distance, a car. This time, I wasn't going to blow it.

I jumped up and ran into the road, waving my arms wildly until the car drew closer, honked furiously, and finally came to a shrieking, skidding stop. It was a dusty-white minivan with a woman at the wheel, her hand cupped against her forehead.

Mrs. Lorrey—peering back at me.

She jabbed at her seatbelt and stumbled out of the car. She was wearing an oversized Britney Spears t-shirt and pink sweatpants. Marianne's clothes. Her hair was a mess of curls, her face in heavy makeup, deep wrinkles at each corner of her downturned mouth.

She trotted toward me, shuffling in strappy pink heels. Again, she cupped her hand to her forehead, though I was easy enough to see in her headlights.

"Marty, is that you?"

"Yeah, it's me."

"I could have killed you in the road like that." When she leaned in to hug me, she winced—I was that cold. I smelled her perfume, a cloud of alcohol and cigarettes.

"Where were you?" I asked.

She sighed into my flannel shirt.

"Where were *you*?" she asked, almost shouting.

"In the field."

"Doing what?"

I shrugged. "I don't know, nothing."

"Well, that's what I was doing, too."

"Aren't you supposed to be in Georgia?"

"I'm back. Back for a minute. Walter, that son of a bitch, booked rooms at Madam Maagimy's, so everyone's gone from the house, even Marianne. He said he was being nice, giving me space to pack the rest of my shit, his words not mine. Well, screw him, right? I'm not going to sit alone in that dark, dismal house." She pulled away from me, fighting to stand still. "Where should we go instead?"

I thought about saying *Florida*. Even Georgia would get me close enough; I could catch a bus from there. But there was a problem: it was late, and she'd sober up before we reached Illinois. And this whole plan would fall apart.

I led Mrs. Lorrey back to the van and helped her into the passenger's seat.

"Ooooh." She laughed maniacally. "Where we going?" From far enough away, we probably looked like runaway teenagers. Off to a Britney Spears concert.

Mrs. Lorrey was asleep before I pulled onto the highway.

The dash read 2:29 a.m. As we passed the junkyard, nearing the stretch of highway along the cliffs, she startled awake. She looked out the window, confused and rubbing her eyes, turning her makeup into full raccoon.

She looked surprised to see me. "Oh, Marty. When did you learn to drive? Did your father teach you?"

She reached across my seat to straighten the line of my seatbelt. "It seems like yesterday you girls were just fourteen."

"I'm thirteen."

She either hiccupped or burped. "But you're driving?"

"Yeah, driving you home."

Mrs. Lorrey flicked off her heels and tucked her feet beneath her. She closed her eyes. Her lips moved, but she said nothing.

"What are you doing? Talking to yourself?" I said.

She shook her head.

"Praying? Could you teach me?"

"What for? It doesn't work." Her voice was abrasive, too loud for the van. "Maybe you should ask Alicia. She's the new CCD leader in Laurel—did you hear that? She took my husband. My house. Now my job. They've got her picture up inside the church. Volunteer of the Month. You know who they never picked?"

"I could guess."

She dug her nails into the dash.

When we finally reached her house, she said, "Stay over. You've got your pick of empty rooms."

"I should get home," I said, though it was the last place I wanted to go.

I helped Mrs. Lorrey to the front door. She leaned into me, her warm hair pressed against my head. "Oh, and Marty." She fumbled with her house key. "I wasn't going to say anything. No, your father asked me not to. But one night—I don't know—in the winter, near the first snow, I saw your mother in the woods behind my house."

"My mother?"

Her sleepy eyes roamed the dark lawn. "She was making a big scene. Arguing. Angry at your father as usual."

"What happened? Where'd she go?"

"I looked away for a second, and they were gone."

"You're sure it was her?"

"You can't mistake a woman like that." She leaned against the front door. "Your father told me not to tell. He was embarrassed, I think."

"About what?"

"Being left behind. You know exactly what I'm talking about. The thing about your mom was that she was *special*—at least she thought so. Too good for him. Too good for you."

I let that slide. "Could you hear them? What were they saying?"

"What do you think? She comes back only to leave again." She turned the key and stumbled into her house. I thought about following her inside, asking again what they were arguing about and where she might've gone, but Mrs. Lorrey was useless, another one of my father's sympathizers. She dropped her heels and belly-flopped onto the couch.

I felt sick on the walk back to Sylvia's. I couldn't tell whether I was happy or horrified that another person had seen my mother. That she had been here. And gone where? Dad had probably kicked her out while I was sleeping. Sent her away. Lied about that, too. Tried to make me feel crazy, saying I'd imagined her.

By now, I knew he was capable of lying, of carrying on for years, but this was different. He had manipulated me, tortured me with her absence. Watched me search for her for weeks, fret around the house for years wondering why she'd stopped calling, stopped writing, didn't care.

He was so far from the person I'd imagined he was. Sure, he had always been quiet, almost eerily so, and he'd kept to himself, but Dad was strong, reliable, the kind of person who could make you laugh unexpectedly, though that was rare now. The kind of person who did things the right way, the hard way. Simple and unassuming. A person everyone admired. I had admired him, too. For sticking around and trying his best to talk to me, trying to be both father and mother, when you could tell it was the most uncomfortable thing in the world.

It was awful seeing him exposed. There was something mean in him. He was still lying. Mom was out there. An outcast, who needed me. And I had failed her. I couldn't believe how ridiculous I'd been, running away like some brat looking for attention.

I should've saved up money. Made plans. Gotten farther than five miles out of town. Gone from motel to motel, asking bored receptionists about a woman with yellow hair, hardly any money, who probably acted like she had more. They had to remember my mother, that false ring in her voice when she called them *darling*, nervous eyes, the way she fumbled with her purse, was most likely short at checkout but still managed to make them feel small. I could've asked what they knew; they might've known where she'd gone. I could've followed her, seven years later, all the way to Florida. I could've figured out where she was living now.

CHAPTER SIXTEEN

Marta

Dad and Sylvia came back in the frozen starry hours before dawn. I was curled up on my cot, listening to the clock chime by the quarter hour, dreading the moment they would walk in. Eventually, the door hinge groaned and the lights flipped on. I heard Dad and Sylvia settle into the kitchen; they argued in hushed, angry voices over whether or not they should wake me up.

"She can't do this," Dad said. "We went all the way to the island, filed a police report. She made me sick. And look at you."

"I'm fine," Sylvia said. "Everything's fine."

"I'm sick."

I could hear wet boots on linoleum and Sylvia's *hush, hush.*

"Don't wake her. It's only gonna make her more upset," she said.

"She *should* be more upset. She deserves to be."

"Just phone the sheriff. Let him know."

"She can't do this."

I could hear a rustling of bodies, of soaked, dripping fabric. The light above the stove was on, but from my cot I could barely see over the kitchen counter. They were standing there like two drowned rats, Dad leaning over the sink and Sylvia using a dish towel to dry her hair. Her light pink blouse was soaked and see-through, clinging to her skin. She combed her hair back with her fingers. Took a deep breath like she'd been holding it in all night.

Dad blew air into his hands. "Look at my fingers. They're bone white."

"Quiet." Sylvia reached around him and turned the faucet on. "Run them under hot water."

"I can't feel them."

"You'll survive."

They didn't speak again. There was silence, only interrupted by the running water and Dad's labored breath. I closed my eyes but did not sleep. Sylvia crept by my cot—it was impossible to breathe normally when someone was watching you pretend to sleep—and Dad stayed in the kitchen, grieving in sharp, quiet breaths. It felt good to hurt him, even in this small way. Nothing compared to how he had hurt me.

In the morning, I found Dad slumped against the stove, legs outstretched, two puddles beneath his dripping work boots. His skin looked yellowish against the mustard-colored linoleum, and he was snoring as loud as a bear. I tiptoed around him, found the remnants of a week-old Berry Merry pie, and ate from the tin, careful not to make noise.

I grabbed a damp washcloth from the sink and slinked into the bathroom. I had scratched myself pretty badly last night when I was lying in the grass. Thin red lines cut through the freckles on my face. With a finger I traced one scratch, starting at the curling baby hairs on my left temple and following it all the way down to my chin—a tender, searing hook. I worked soap into the washcloth and dabbed it against my skin. It burned. The sink in Sylvia's bathroom was still broken so I cranked on the bathtub faucet to rinse the rag. That was when I heard the ancient croak of her bedsprings.

I locked the bathroom door and sat down on the cool tile, leaning against the tub.

There was a gentle knock.

"Marty. Are you all right?" She twisted the doorknob.

"I'm fine."

"I saw the marks on your face."

I waited.

"You can talk to me. I won't say anything to your dad," she said.

"Will too."

"Will not."

"Go back to bed."

The door creaked—it sounded like she was leaning on it, probably hoping I would change my mind and let her in.

"Please," I said.

I heard her slippers drag away from the door, across the living room.

CHAPTER SEVENTEEN

Marta

For the next few days I skipped school. I woke up early, took the ferry to the island. Stood there in the woods, looking up at my house. It looked skeletal, a few windows left open, nothing inside. I couldn't bring myself to try the door. I sat on the cold porch and watched the trees bend and knew this was the last time. I wouldn't come back here.

I had an urge to go to Mrs. Lorrey, to sit beside her in my mother's house. If she hadn't been such a mess, she might've helped me. Felt sorry enough to slip me some cash. Let me stay with her until I found my mom. It was strange how repulsed I was by Mrs. Lorrey, how much I felt I needed her. Sylvia was the only person I really had.

I went to the diner and sat at the counter. Jaybird shot me a look from the grill. He flipped a pancake. "Shouldn't you be at school?" he asked. I knew he was on Sylvia's side. She had probably been crying at the diner, saying it was my fault.

When I turned to watch Sylvia work, Jaybird did, too. She was cleaning up after the bridge club, wiping down their sticky playing cards, pausing only to rub at her red swollen eyes. She looked exhausted. She'd been working doubles since Dad and I'd moved in. Taking bartending shifts at the Midnight Girls for extra cash. I imagined her slinging beers down the counter, glaring at the dancers, their perfect bodies and easy tips. Nothing had come easily to Sylvia. But there was something magnetic in the way she moved—though her speed was glacial. Systematically clearing dishes, swiping crumbs into the palm of her hand. Reinstating a little order after other people had created a mess.

Jaybird tapped his spatula against the grill. *Tink-tink-tink.* He pointed the spatula at my face. "Whatever you're doing, you'd better stop."

I flipped back my hair and called for Sylvia. She hurried over, four dirty plates balanced on her forearms, and shrugged the dishes into the wash bin.

"Cherry pop?" I asked as nicely as I could.

For the first time in months, Sylvia smiled. She rushed over to the pop machine, shoveling in maraschino cherries as the cup filled and overfilled.

Jaybird sighed, pushing through the swinging doors into the kitchen. He'd left the pancakes burning on the grill. Even before now, I'd felt he hated me. Probably assumed I didn't pay, which was technically true.

Sylvia wiped the glass and slid it down the counter to me. The bell above the door rang, but she ignored it, paying no mind to the family of tourists coming into the diner. They hesitated near the door, glancing around, waiting for Sylvia to notice them. Instead, she sat next to me.

Eventually, the father became brave. He picked up a menu from next to the cash register, and the family gathered around it. The eldest, a grandmother in a rain bonnet, couldn't read it without glasses and broke away, groping her way along the dessert case, tapping her cane at each pie beneath the glass. I watched as the family's three children started to scramble around the empty booths, plucking brochures from wall racks and using them to sword-fight. After what seemed like forever, Jaybird reemerged from the kitchen, glaring at me and then the children. He said nothing to Sylvia, seating the family himself.

I sipped my pop. Sylvia pulled out a notebook, turned to a page covered in red tallies, and starting counting, the tip of her pen tapping each mark.

She drew a sharp line across the page, wrote "88," and circled the number. "You've been gone for eighty-eight days," she said.

"I haven't gone anywhere."

"Well, you haven't been here. Not for eighty-eight days."

"Hasn't been that long."

"Maybe longer." Sylvia ripped the page from the notebook and chucked it into the wash bin. "Maybe, some days, I forgot to count."

"I walk by all the time."

"You never come inside. You know, Jesus only disappeared for three days."

I blew bubbles into my pop.

"Three," she repeated. "And he had a pretty good reason."

"I was avoiding Dad."

"Me, Marty. After everything I've done for you. The dinners I've made. A mountain of laundry." She was pouting.

"Fine, from you. Because you were after him—it was obvious. Touching his jeans under the table. Sleeping in my mother's bed."

Her face looked hot. "I never touched her room."

"You bleached your hair. You were trying to make him love you. It was working."

Sylvia let out a short, injured laugh. "Wake up, Marty. He loves you. Loves Glory." Her voice peaked at the G and dragged out slowly, as if the air were being knocked out of her lungs.

Relief washed over me, cool and kind but, like summer rain, passing far too quickly. I was left with a heat wave of shame, a feeling far worse than seeing my dress on another girl. I had wanted to hurt Sylvia. I hadn't realized she had already been hurting.

She stood up, wiping at the coffee grounds on her apron.

I reached out and touched her hand. "He lied to both of us," I said, putting on my best performance. "He forced her to go."

The story spilled out. How Mom had been back for just one night and had disappeared after Dad had come home. How he told me it had all been a dream, that she had never come back and never would. But she *had* come back. Mrs. Lorrey had seen them fighting in the woods behind her house. Something bad had happened. He was hiding something. Just like he'd hidden everything in the burn pile.

Sylvia gripped the counter as if bracing herself. "Well, where is she now?"

Some place in the south with alligators in the backyard, orange blossoms as white as snow. Wherever she was, she missed me. Though she'd never said it, I told Sylvia that Mom missed her, too. And that she wanted to come home but didn't have any money.

Sylvia pressed her hand against her stomach, her face pale as the moon. "I don't understand. She wants to come back *here*?"

"Here."

"And she misses me?"

"You," I said, nodding fiercely.

"I have savings, money from my parents," she said, pulling out her notebook. "I was saving for a down payment." She scribbled a number, then paused. "No, he'd never forgive me."

"I need your help."

"Please, Marty. I can't get involved."

"I've got no one."

"Yeah." She had this sad, distant look in her eyes. "That I know."

"You've got to search through Dad's stuff. Maybe he's hiding a phone number. An address. We've got to find her."

"This would be the end."

"Of what?"

Sylvia looked at me sharply. She was a strong woman but fragile, too, something she didn't want anyone to know. "I'll see what I can do. I'll talk to your daddy."

I squeezed her hand. "You can't tell him anything."

When she didn't respond, I said, "Promise me."

"She misses me? She said that?"

"Don't you miss her, too?"

Sylvia pressed her knuckles to her lips. Let out a big sigh. "More than you know."

On Monday, I went back to school. I slung my backpack onto the floor and sat down at the desk closest to Mr. Purdy, to make things easier for him. I knew he would hover over me like a nurse. Over the course of a single hour, he laid out all of the assignments and tests I had missed, helping me fill in answers and hinting *true* or *false* instead of teaching the rest of the class. They had a silent reading period, though no one was reading. Marianne painted her nails. She looked up once and smiled at me. The rest of the girls ignored me, like the old days.

Levi ignored me, too. No note. Nothing. Maybe because I'd ditched him too many times. Or maybe he'd lost interest. I'd heard that he was hanging out with another girl. Her family owned Sweet Caroline Inn, where all our best silverware had gone after the yard sale. She must've been special. The inn was named after her.

After school, I saw them sitting at the end of the dock where we used to meet, their bare feet dangling over the water. They were whispering. I watched Levi slip his hand inside her shiny, expensive-looking raincoat, resting his thumb against her spine. I felt the ghost of that warm pressure on my own back. I wanted to run down and shove them both off the dock.

I was seething, but I lingered. Taking after Sylvia.

I watched as Caroline leaned forward, over the water, and Levi quickly kissed the back of her neck. As I walked back to Sylvia's, I could see the kiss over and over as if it were my only memory. That night with Levi in the kitchen no longer existed. I no longer existed. It was a strange feeling, feeling sorry for yourself but knowing you had it coming. I had been bad to Levi, like Marianne had said. I had no idea what was going on in his life. Everything had been about me. He had helped me search for my mom. He had brought me her journal and had allowed me to cry in his arms. He had left the homecoming dance. And for what? I'd ignored him. I was just like Mom.

———————

The thaw was over. The water rolled across the channel, around the rocky island—pale green close to shore, pushing into the deepest blue. Still cold as ice. Even in the summer, you'd get hypothermia in minutes if you fell into the middle of the lake. It was far too early for swimmers now. Couples strolled along the beach, their hair whipping up around them, all crazy. Dogs chased waves. I counted dozens of sailboats on the horizon, kayaks tracing the shore. The world was coming back to life—green grass, new leaves, wildflowers springing from ditches. My favorite were the tiny blue phlox blanketing the shoulders of the highway.

The whole town smelled like new earth, pure and quiet. We had a few weeks to ourselves before the tourists came.

Dad was working again, repairing a fence at the apple orchard. While he was out, Sylvia dug through his suitcase but didn't find anything.

I searched Sylvia's bedroom myself and found nothing. Only Dad's tattered jeans, flannels, a double-edged razor, shaving cream, and a single freshwater pearl in the bottom of his suitcase. I took the pearl and slipped it into the front pocket of my jeans.

I was starting to think we'd need to ask him directly to get to Mom, but I knew that wouldn't work. He was selfish, conniving. He would do all he could to keep her away, just like he'd done for the past seven years. Sylvia would have to coax the truth out of him, slowly, carefully, when he was least expecting it.

CHAPTER EIGHTEEN

Marta

"Don't make a fuss," Sylvia said, straightening Dad's collar. "She's too old for a sitter."

"But she needs one," he said. "Otherwise we'd come home to an empty house. And I'd have to call the sheriff again. He already thinks I'm a lousy father."

"He didn't say that."

"He didn't have to."

He meant his record. The DUIs. The reason I walked pretty much everywhere.

As Sylvia smoothed the wrinkles in his shirt, Dad arched his body away from her. I had never seen him wear his good church clothes outside of church. She struggled to button his shirt with her long stick-on nails. He swatted her hands away when she reached his chin.

Sylvia had made reservations at Madam Maagimy's, the town's most romantic restaurant, though it didn't have much competition. A fancy date night wasn't what I'd had in mind when I'd asked Sylvia to pry, but I could tell she was happy, all dolled up in her wispy silk dress. Her eyes matched the color of the dress, dark plum. She had dyed her hair red again, an apology to me. It wasn't the same shade as her roots, but her burgundy hair shone brightly under the kitchen lights. She looked prettier than she ever had before. I felt terrible. Ashamed of Dad for leaning away from her. Ashamed of myself for the relief it gave me.

"Your belt," she reminded him. "And you need your dress shoes."

"Don't need 'em," he said, leaning over the kitchen sink.

He worked soap into his coarse stubble, then made quick, neat strokes with his razor. The shaving cream fell sharply into the sink, plops of snow.

Dad didn't trust me to walk over to Onie's myself. So, after shaving, he grabbed my wrist and walked me there in silence. He'd been like this for weeks. He wouldn't talk to me and barely spoke to Sylvia. I came home from school to an empty apartment. He was working at the orchards, at night plumbing toilets at local motels. He was brooding, exhausted, growing years older with each graveyard shift.

We curved right at the bottom of the mainland hill and started weaving through beach bungalows until we found Onie's. Among a row of pretty houses, her peach bungalow shrugged under the fading sun. The winter had been hard on her house. Cracks ran up and down the siding. The gray-green shutters fell away from the windows, unhinged at the top. Dad cleared dirt from the front window with the sleeve of his good shirt and looked inside.

"What happened to this place?" he said.

"She lives up there." I pointed at the second story. "It's a duplex."

"It's one house. I laid the foundation. Hung the drywall."

I had visited Onie plenty of times with Mom. I had seen her about the dress last December. There was the staircase, steep and creaky, and the sewing room packed with giant machines and heaps of fabric. Her bedroom, next to her sewing room, was the size of a walk-in closet. It only had room for a twin bed and a nightstand, which was crowded with wedding pictures— one, two, three like dominoes. A photo for each marriage.

"The lower level's boarded off from the stairs," I said.

Dad jogged along the perimeter of the yard. He checked the windows around the side, the French doors at the back of the house. There were white sheets hanging so you couldn't see anything. The backyard was chaos—buckets, rain gauges, decapitated soda bottles scattered in the tall grass. Dad frowned at his church slacks and knelt in the grass. He picked up a bottle.

"Her third husband used to measure the rain. He was studying at home. Trying to steal the weatherman's job," he said.

I heard Onie calling me from the porch.

"She's out front," I said. I nudged one of the buckets with my foot until it toppled over.

"Don't." Dad lunged to pick it back up. "She's *particular*. You can't go around touching his things."

"Whose things?"

"Gene's. He left her, wanted to go back to school. He was eighty-two years old."

Onie came around the side of the house. She was wearing a loose nightgown, her long grey hair looped into a low bun. She stepped carefully over fat puddles.

"Upstairs," she said to me.

"Everything okay with the house?" Dad asked her.

Onie flicked her wrist. "You ought to go." She might have been the only woman in town who didn't like him.

He stood up, swatting at the wet grass stains on his knees. The khaki fabric was stained with earth. Sylvia would be embarrassed to take him to supper like that.

It was obvious he was stalling.

"She's waiting," Onie said. "You gonna make that woman wait forever."

He matted the grass with his heel. "It's just, I noticed the sheets covering the doors."

She leaned down, bones creaking, and grabbed the bucket I had tipped. "Someone's been messing with his water. He's not going to like it."

"You mean Gene?"

"Who else."

"So he *is* coming back?" Dad said.

She smiled. "Time to go."

Finally he did, and we were alone in the yard. Onie slinked

around, measuring rain levels. While her back was turned, I hurried to the French doors and wiped clean a space on the glass. Between two hanging bedsheets, I saw a sliver of the first floor. Dirty dishes in the sink, a full coffee pot, an iron left out, a man's shirt draped across an ironing board, half a sandwich sitting on top of a textbook. The sandwich fuzzy with mold. Somehow the television was still on. It was like she was trying to preserve the house. Keep everything in place. Board it off until he waltzed back in. This was how she waited for Gene, and I felt sorry for her, like I'd felt sorry for Mrs. Lorrey. And for myself.

"It's going to rain today," she said. "At least four inches."

I looked up. "There aren't any clouds."

It rained five inches by sundown. When I asked how she'd known, if she could tell by the buckets or by how the wind was blowing, she smirked, "Indians watch the forecast, too. We get the same stations."

She brought me up to her sewing room, stashed me on the floor next to a heap of powder-pink tulle, and told me to gather skirts. The first-grade ballerinas needed costumes for their next dance recital. I did the work slowly, slipping elastic through the waistbands with a safety pin, slide-gathering until sheets of tulle were bound up in circles. She sat at her sewing desk and flipped on a blinding desk lamp. Though the leotards were tiny, it would take hours, she told me, to sequin hearts on all fifteen. I would learn something from her efforts, she said. How to work hard, something I clearly hadn't learned in school. Apparently, Onie had seen me walking out to the ferry's loading dock, playing hooky.

"She didn't raise you, but it didn't matter," Onie said. "You're just like Glory."

Hearing her name felt sharper than a needle. "You don't really know her," I said.

"Better than you do. I made all her dresses. Baptism, first communion, confirmation, wedding. Every pageant. Sylvia's, too. And you know what? I worked harder on Sylvia's. Lace. Embroidery. Bead work. But it didn't matter, she never won."

"Because my mom was prettier."

"On the outside, sure."

I pushed the elastic through the waistband and gathered too hard, shredding the tulle.

"You know, you were lucky she left." Onie tied off a heart of sequins and split the thread between her teeth. "Really, she was rotten. Bad to Sylvia."

"Who cares about Sylvia."

"Bad to your father. Bad to everyone."

"Everybody loved her." I tried to say it coolly. "Dad thought he was the luckiest guy in town." A long time ago, before he was bitter, Dad had talked about Mom like she was a prize he had won. The other guys had tried to win her heart. Girls had been envious. None more than Sylvia. Mom was special. She didn't just think she was better than everyone else. She was.

"Lucky?" Onie scoffed.

Defeated, miserable, I sat there in the corner. I couldn't believe what Onie had said about my mother. What did she have against her? Mom was beautiful. That wasn't her fault. Maybe she was cold sometimes, slipping a cigarette between her lips to avoid a conversation. Maybe distant, a loner like me. But not rotten. She was better than Dad, better than anyone I knew.

Maybe not better. Misunderstood. Misplaced on that frozen island. Angry and difficult and terrible for doing what she'd done. But she was mine. *My* mother.

"I hurt your feelings," Onie said. "But someone had to tell you. And wouldn't you rather know? Some kids never really know their parents, and now, at least, you know a little something about your mom."

"You want me to thank you?" My voice was hot.

"You could. Now you won't miss her."

"You're old and you're crazy. I miss her every time I look at Dad, at this lake, at this stupid town, any girl laughing with her mother—I hate them—and I even miss her when I look at you, when you say she was rotten. I missed her even when she was around." I remembered those days cooped up in the house with her, when she'd sit on the bathroom floor with one of her headaches, door locked, running the faucet. So she could cry, so we wouldn't hear her. But, of course, we did. A paralyzing sound. And when she finally came out, she'd walk past us like we weren't in the room. She saw nothing, heard nothing. Cringed at my touch. Even back then, I ached for her.

"Well, I wish someone would tell me Gene was bad. So I didn't miss him."

"He left you. Doesn't that say enough?"

"You tell me." She smirked, and I felt the weight of it.

I wanted to go home, back to Sylvia's crowded apartment, to my cot in the dining room, where I could sleep and dream of Mom—a rare smile, a kiss on the temple.

The longer Onie stared at me, the more her eyes softened. "I loved your mother. She was awful in a way. I know everyone tells you that. I know it doesn't make it easier. She was always sad. That's what I remember most about her. And I remember how angry that made me, this little girl who had everything and everyone. I expected more from her—she should look me in the eyes when she came to collect a dress, ask a single question. She would stand there in the corner where you're sitting now, waiting with her mother's checkbook. Gloomy, silent. In public she was always performing, but to me she was this empty vessel."

That was exactly how she had felt at home.

"What happened to Gene?" I said, knowing it was time I asked.

She looked surprised. "I'm sure he's dead. He was dying when he left. He told me there was no more time to waste. I suppose he meant on me."

"I'm sorry."

"You know the feeling." She smiled. "It isn't goodbye, you know. In Ojibwe we don't have that word. It's Giga-waabamin miinawaa—I'll see you again."

CHAPTER NINETEEN

Sylvia

It was midnight. Sylvia slipped off her heels and walked home with Bo from Madam Maagimy's. His body was heavy against hers, weighed down by his stumbling sadness. She felt that sadness, too. Nothing had come out at dinner. He had complained about the menu, drunk five whiskey sours, one after the other, and only touched her now when he needed help walking home.

All these months they'd been together, he had never kissed her. Never slept in her bed.

"I can't go back," he said, almost shouting. "Let's look at the stars. Lie down on the dock."

"There's not a star in the sky."

"Let's get Marty. She loves a meteor shower."

Sylvia sighed deeply. "You're drunk. You can't see Marty. Better if she stays with Onie tonight."

Bo staggered forward into the road, running and teetering until he was a block ahead of her, a blur disappearing into the low curve of the hill. The road was skinny and dark, stretched out like a river flowing from the old chapel into the big lake. Anything but smooth. In Sylvia's lifetime, the pavement had never been repaired. It had potholes big enough to break ankles, tree roots tunneling underfoot. From the sidewalk, Sylvia watched as Bo tripped over one of those roots in the road and plunged headfirst into the darkness.

As Sylvia ran over, the rocky pavement shredded her nylons. The panic ruined her hair. Bo was lying on the ground when she reached him. He wasn't hurt, only embarrassed, laughing when he discovered he couldn't stand up alone. Sylvia helped him from the street up the stairs to her apartment. She washed the pressed gravel from his hands—they were bleeding—led him to the bedroom, and pushed him onto her bed. Dead weight. She pulled off his work boots.

He looked up at her sweetly. "I'm sorry. I haven't had a drink since Glory left."

"Sure." Sylvia had been surprised when he'd ordered drinks at dinner, but now she was starting to suspect that his sobriety was over.

"I swear I'll get you back for rent."

"Stay as long as you want."

He smiled sleepily and rolled onto his side. Sylvia folded the comforter over him, making a cocoon. He was pathetic like this. She could hardly stand to look at him.

"The money's coming," he said.

Her back ached from lugging Bo up the stairs. Her silk dress clung to her sweaty, cold skin. She yanked her torn nylons down, freeing her waist, and plucked them off her feet. She wriggled out of her dress. Freedom, finally.

She washed her face with cold water, shimmied into a clean, crisp set of pajamas, and lay down on Bo's inflatable camping mat. The nylon stuck to the bare parts of her skin and squeaked every time she moved. She felt monstrous, even after all that dieting and exercise. Carrying those weights around like a moron. Everyone in town had probably laughed at her for trying so hard, as if trying to change meant you thought you were better than other people. "Look at her go," she imagined them saying. In small towns, there was nothing more embarrassing than being accused of liking yourself a little too much. Not that she had that problem.

"It's coming. Soon as I sell the storage." Bo was speaking, but she couldn't tell if he were awake.

"What's coming?" Her voice was soft.

"The storage shed."

Sylvia sprang up, sat on edge of the bed. "What storage?"

He snored, warm and rattling.

She nudged his shoulder. He made a lazy effort to shove her off the bed. She elbowed him in the side. He was still strong, firm across the middle.

"The storage. Clear some things," he said. "A couple hundred bucks."

"Where's the storage? What road?"

He was asleep again.

She pulled back the comforter and searched his pockets. Nothing but a few receipts. Groceries from Lucy's, tackle from the rez. In the back pockets, a worn leather wallet with two school pictures of Marty, ages five and nine, and one of Glory at their wedding, standing in front the chapel alone. A ring of keys. Three keys, two marked—"Cellar," "Sylvia A"—the third a blank skeleton key, ancient and rusty. Sylvia slipped that key off the ring and wedged the others back into his pocket. She refolded the comforter over Bo.

A minute later, she was kicking up sand on the shore, sprinting up Onie's front porch.

She rang the doorbell once, seven times.

She yelled, "Marty!" until the bungalows next door blinked with lights.

Finally, the stairs creaked and the door swung open. Onie stood there, with Marty sitting on the stairs behind her. It was strange—Marty looked happy to see Sylvia.

"Sylvia, your clothes," Onie said, frowning.

Sylvia hadn't realized that she was wearing her slippers, legs bare in silky pajama shorts. "I'm here to get Marty," she said.

Onie crossed her arms. "It's late. And you've been drinking."

"I'm fine."

"Sylvia." Onie's voice was mean, her face knitted with anger.

"I need to talk to her," Sylvia said, just as mean. "Look at me. I'm good."

There was a long pause. A hard stare. Commotion in a neighbor's bungalow. People were watching from a bedroom window. Onie sighed.

"Take her home," she said to Marty. "Make sure she doesn't fall."

Marty took Sylvia's hand and led her down the porch steps, along the shore. Though it was forty degrees, Sylvia could feel herself sweating.

She said, "There's something I need to tell you. Something I found."

CHAPTER TWENTY

Marta

Sylvia was skunk-drunk, glossy-eyed with smudged mascara. She could walk a line, tell the water from the shore, but her pajamas were on backward, neckline jutting low, silk buttons down her back, the drawstring springing like a pig's tail from her tailbone. Her face glowed under the roaming lighthouse beacon. Her short red hair twisted in the wind.

"He's never gonna speak to me again," she said. She was holding something; she was walking with her arms extended, cupping whatever it was like a trapped bug.

"Tell me what happened," I said.

She looked around, checking the bungalows along the beach and then glancing up at the lightless town. Around us, mosquitoes buzzed. In the morning, we would wake up covered with welts, bites split open, blood on ankles and sheets.

"Come on," I said.

Sylvia made a doorway with her thumbs. "Be quiet."

My eyes took a few seconds to adjust, before I could see what she was holding. It was a skeleton key. "So what?"

She closed her hands around it. "Don't say anything. I could get thrown in jail."

"For what?"

She looked around again, suspicious of the midnight waves that inched toward our feet. "I took this from your dad. He doesn't know we have it."

"What's it for? A safe-deposit box?"

"No."

"A safe?"

"No."

"Spit it out."

"A storage garage. He's about to sell it off."

My breath felt sharp. It was true then. He was hiding something. Sylvia had found him out.

"It's probably nothing," she said, circling me. "Probably some carpentry tools, lumber."

"He's got his stuff at the orchard."

"It's empty. I'm sure."

"No."

"Probably just a bunch of old furniture that didn't sell."

"Everything sold."

Sylvia pressed the cool metal into my hand. "It's nothing." Her voice was high, strained. "Let's just go home. Slip the key back onto his keyring."

"We have to look before he wakes up. He gets up early when he's been drinking."

"He hasn't been drinking."

"Sylvia." Surely she knew. She couldn't be that dumb. Yes, he had chips from AA. He had taken breaks from drinking for a month, for three months at a time. He called himself sober. But those breaks were interludes. "He never stopped."

Sylvia looked at me like her heart was sinking. She really was that dumb.

"Let's go," I said.

She took my hand and led me up the hill, to the alley behind Jaybird's. His baby-blue Thunderbird was parked behind the dumpster, spare key in the visor. Sylvia climbed in. "He said I could borrow it for emergencies. Seatbelt."

Mine was broken, but I pretended to fasten it. She was drunk, but I needed her to drive. I was too nervous. My skin was beaded with sweat. What did I expect to find out there? Junk, maybe furniture from my grandparents' house? Couches covered in plastic? What was I hoping for? Some clue—an address, another letter, something that would lead me to her.

Sylvia crept along the alleyway, no headlights. I didn't look up until we crested the hill. The chapel glowed under the heavy yellow moon. The stars were gone, and the tombstones behind the chapel loomed like hacked tree stumps.

Suddenly Sylvia let go of the clutch, and we stalled out by the graveyard. "This is stupid. There's nothing out here. We don't even know where we're going."

"There's only one storage garage on 13." We both knew. It was a few miles away.

"This is crazy. I've had too much to drink."

"Let's go."

"We're going back."

"Now." My voice was hot.

She restarted the engine, pumped the clutch, and shifted into first.

The highway coiled around the back of the mainland hill, bent in sharply at the shore, and then dragged out along the coast, heading toward the rez. Sylvia drove slowly—much too slowly, especially near the cliffs. I could tell she was nervous. I knew she regretted giving me the key. She was probably regretting her whole life, everything up to this moment.

I was nervous too. I pressed my face against the cool window and tried to calm down. We passed the lake, then the hoarder's junkyard. Before us, the Red Cliff reservation opened up like a spring bloom, the general store to the right, a handful of cottages and campgrounds hidden in the trees, and the VFW bar that was always open. The town of Red Cliff was several miles long, sparse and wooded. Birch trees and giant white pines lined the highway. A huge casino sat next to the water, then a white church with a bright red roof, and, beyond that, the storage garage—close to where they held the powwows.

"Turn here," I said.

Sylvia rubbed her eyes. Mascara was running down her cheeks, shimmering in the weak light of the dashboard. She had been crying. I slid the key into the pocket of my jeans and reached across the car. I touched her arm.

"You think we're going to find something?" I asked.

"No."

"You're crying."

"It's nothing."

"I don't feel good either."

"He'll never forgive me." She wiped her sleeve across her nose.

"He won't know a thing."

"He'll know."

"I won't say."

"It won't matter."

"You said it yourself, he doesn't even love—"

"Don't say that, Marty. Please don't."

She took the turn too sharply, and we plunged into a ditch. She cursed and struck the wheel with her palm, saying, "Don't, don't, don't." The car had stalled, and now she restarted the engine, revving it, kicking up weeds and sending mud flying, but it was no use: we were stuck. The engine wheezed and the wheels lurched back and forth, rutting us deeper into the ground. She cursed again.

"Anyway, we're here," I said.

Sylvia cranked the car key, again and again, but the starter refused to catch. She pressed her forehead against the steering wheel, fully defeated.

"Let's go. We'll worry about the car later," I said.

"It's too late."

"It's not past one."

"It's over, Marty."

"Not even close."

"For me."

"I'm sorry. Really."

"You shouldn't have asked me."

"There was no one else."

Sylvia straightened up, leaning back against the seat. She flipped down the visor and studied her face in the mirror.

"Geez, look at me," she said, dragging her finger under her eyes and collecting mascara. "I look crazy. I was acting crazy." She flipped the mirror up quickly. "But you're fine now," she said to herself.

I popped the passenger door and stumbled into the night, slipping a few times in the mud. Sylvia moved slowly, slippers careful in the ditch. She almost looked sober.

"This way," I called.

Most of the garage doors were shut without locks, a few hanging open, buried in dead leaves. Five of them were locked, and only one had an antique padlock. I slid the skeleton key into the barrel, twisted the bow to the left, and the shackle popped open. Too easy. If there had been something to hide, he would have tried harder to conceal it.

"Go on, open it," Sylvia said. "Don't be scared."

She lifted the shackle from the latch and yanked up the screeching metal door. There it was: a tiny square slab of concrete, swept clean, not a scuff or a mark on the walls. The space was empty except for a single white bedsheet heaped in the corner.

"I told you," Sylvia said, clapping.

Relief.

The wind pushed through my hair and into that small space of the garage. I could smell new paint. I stepped into the moonlit space and swiped my fingers against the walls. They were sticky, wet.

I moved to the back corner, where the sheet lay, all twisted up.

"We should get going. It's late to be out here," Sylvia said.

I picked up the sheet, pulled until it slinked away from the wall. There was weight to it, movement. I knew there was something in there, and it clattered to the ground.

A purse.

A glossy pink satchel. This purse. Hers. That December morning. The moment I saw her. A wave of yellow hair. Orange stockings. Pink coat. Pink purse slipping down her arm.

I dropped the sheet.

Sylvia didn't move.

I knelt before the purse and worked the clasp apart. The mouth sprang open and there, just as I had remembered them, were all my mother's things: her little pink wallet, an empty pack of cigarettes, dark copper-colored lipstick. Jujubes floating at the bottom, hard as rocks. Inside her wallet was her driver's license from 1991, two pictures of herself, one as a baby, one from a pageant, a wrinkled social security card, four credit cards, and $13.55. I cradled the purse and breathed in the scent of the liner. It was lilac and Virginia Slims.

I felt like throwing up but couldn't. The sickness stayed inside, churning waves in my stomach until I felt so heavy, so flooded, I could no longer stand. Sylvia caught me in her arms, pressed her chin against the top of my head. I held out the purse to her, but she wouldn't touch it.

"It's nothing." She tried to keep her voice even, but it was shrill.

"He's done something."

"It's only a purse."

"Something to her."

"He wouldn't do a thing."

"Why else would he paint the walls?"

"He couldn't."

"You're scared, too. You're shaking."

"Marty, please, for the love of God, don't."

Somehow we made it back to the car. Head spinning, I climbed into the driver's seat, turned the key, pumped the sticky clutch, and shifted into first. As Sylvia shoved all of her weight against the bumper, I let out the clutch slowly, revving the engine. After a few stalls and restarts, the tires finally caught the earth, and the car leapt from the ditch. Jaybird's baby blue was covered in red mud. There was mud in Sylvia's hair, on her clean white pajamas. She'd lost her slippers in the ditch.

She slid into the passenger seat, kicked her bare feet up onto the dash, and leaned her head against the window, just as I had done. Her fingers trembled against her thighs. I held the purse between my knees as I drove.

"She probably left it behind years ago," Sylvia said into the window. "She's always been careless. Forgetful." Her voice was building in certainty; she was trying to convince herself. "Or maybe she didn't want to be Glory from the island. Yeah, that's it. You know, ditch her purse, her name, everything. Start over."

"She had the purse when I saw her. This past winter."

Sylvia shook her head. "You're getting confused."

"He's got her license, her cards. She couldn't survive without them."

Sylvia dug her nails into her thigh. "Marty, watch out."

I swerved around a branch on the road. We were moving slowly now, creeping along the black highway. Sylvia stared out the window. I squeezed my knees tightly against the purse. I felt hot, feverish. I followed the headlights around the curve of the lake, hugging the road's inside shoulder to avoid the cliffs. The lake was still, the water a replica of the sky, clouded and dark, the big moon hanging between the island and here.

It was eerie to see the world like that, so undisturbed when we felt otherwise. I hated to see those trees full of ripe green leaves that didn't toss or sway in the wind. The wind didn't come at all. It had swept us into the storage unit and bowed out in a gentle hush. Past the rez, the cicadas died down, and then there was the town, tiny, quiet, and dark, everyone sleeping, breath muted by walls and doors and unopened windows. I wanted to hear them. Anything.

It was past 3 a.m. when we got back home. Dad was asleep, his low, rumbling snore barreling from the bedroom to the kitchen. Sylvia washed her face in the kitchen sink, wiping away the blood-red mud. "Let's go to bed, okay?" She forced a smile. "We can't wake him up now. He's been drinking."

"You can sleep?"

"I didn't say I would sleep, but we could lie down. Or we could watch TV."

"I need to talk to him now."

She wiped the mud from her hair. "We don't need to, not really. He'd tell us what we already know."

"We don't know anything."

"Your daddy is a good man."

"Then wake him up."

The purse felt heavy in my hands. I hooked the pink strap around my arm and let the purse fall to my side. My whole body ached. "What are you so afraid of?"

Sylvia leaned back against the kitchen counter and looked at me, straight at me, for the first time all night. Her eyes were bloodshot and swollen. "Oh, Marty. We've already lost so much."

CHAPTER TWENTY-ONE

Marta

We sat around the dining table, the purse in the center, its contents spilled across the glass surface. Dad was still wearing his good church clothes. His thick black hair was curling from the heat, all of it pushed to one side. His face was marked with the line of a pillowcase. He rubbed his eyes, as if he couldn't quite see what lay before him on the table. Mom's baby picture was face up between his elbows: a heart-shaped face with rosy cheeks, a soft widow's peak, golden hair. He caught his head in his hands and stared down at her. "She used to be so sweet," he said, his breath full of alcohol.

Sylvia shook her head. Apart from her filthy clothes, bare feet, and spiraling red hair, she looked calm.

Dad closed his eyes.

Sylvia nodded at me. "Go on," she mouthed.

"Well?" I said.

His eyes flicked open.

"You better say," Sylvia told him. "This is serious."

"It's four in the morning. What do you want me to say?" Dad flipped over the baby picture. He reached across the table for the picture of Mom in a yellow dress.

"Why do you have it?" I asked as meanly as I could.

"Why did you steal the key?" He matched my tone.

Sylvia cut in, "I took the key. I *borrowed* it after you fell asleep. She didn't do anything."

"Tell me about it. She's an angel."

I grabbed the purse and held the smooth glossy vinyl against my chest.

"You can keep it. I tried and I tried, but she's not coming back," he said.

"You did something," I said.

"Something?"

"To her."

Dad looked from me to Sylvia. "You think I hurt her?" he said, pinching his throat. "I'm dreaming. Drunk."

Sylvia sighed. "Just say why you have it so we can all go to bed."

He laughed, slow and strained. "This is crazy. You're both nuts."

"Bo."

"Don't look at me like that, Sylvia. You're scaring Marty. You've got her all worked up."

"*You* have," Sylvia said. "She's scared of you. We both are."

Dad pressed his fingers against Mom's driver's license. "I'm sorry you think so low of me. Guess I deserve as much."

"Where is she?" I asked.

Dad stared up at the ceiling. "I've done a lot of wrong, Marty. A lot."

"Where?" My voice sounded far away.

"She's not coming. I tried. Lord knows."

"Where?" It was Sylvia this time.

"I called her," he said to me. "I found her number. I had an old address."

"You're lying."

"Tell the truth." Sylvia drummed her fingers on the table.

"I wired her money. She was supposed to come. She promised."

"I don't believe you," I said, scooping up her things from the table. I swept the surface clean and stuffed everything back into her purse.

"I swear. She was living in the Keys in a trailer park." He winced. "She said it's nice."

"You're making this up."

"She was supposed to be here a week ago. I sent $300 for a ticket home."

"You wouldn't do that." I snapped the purse shut and backed away from the table.

"I knew this would happen," he said. "I knew she wouldn't come. I didn't tell you because I couldn't bear to let you down again."

"You were bringing her here?" Sylvia asked. Her question was razor sharp, an accusation.

"Marty needed her." He turned to me. "You needed her. You wanted me to. I sent the money. She swore she'd come."

Sylvia breathed into her hands, head shaking. "Don't lie to her again."

"Give it a rest, Sylvia," he said. "You're the one who's lying."

"You don't know what you're talking about."

"I'm not dumb. I've always known."

"Don't make this about me." Sylvia reached for my hand. "He's trying to twist things. You can see that, can't you?"

"Tell her," he said. "So she can hate you, too."

Dad struck the table. "She's the reason Glory left."

"She wasn't happy," Sylvia cut in, squeezing my hand, hurting me. "It wasn't my fault."

"You egged her on. Gave her money. Kept sending more, hoping she'd disappear for good."

I stared at Sylvia, blank-faced. "You wouldn't do that."

She cringed, and I felt sicker than I'd ever been. I pulled my hand away from her.

Slowly, angrily, she turned to Dad. "You didn't send money to Glory. You have *none*."

"I'll show you the bank receipt." He dug through his wallet. Fumbled through a couple of folded receipts. Nothing from the bank.

Sylvia started to cry. "What did you do to her?"

"Marty," he said, very seriously. "I would never hurt your mom."

"Her purse," I said. "You were hiding it."

"She left it here."

"Why would she do that?"

Dad wouldn't look at me. He pressed his palms against his eyes and waited, maybe hoping we'd all disappear.

Sylvia wiped her face with her sleeve. "Tell her."

He started to cry, too.

I looked at them, both pathetic and red in the face and crying over themselves. I considered for a moment and then flung the purse at Dad's head. It struck the side of his face and fell to the floor.

He touched his jaw. "Please sit down. I'll let you throw it again, ten times, if you'll just sit down." He reached his hand out to me.

I ran—out the door, down the fire escape, straight up the mainland hill. The sun was peeking through the woods. The light was coming. They would find me. I could hear Sylvia's voice, distant but clear. She was shouting. The door slammed. They were coming. I ran past the diner. Up the strip. "Where you going, baby?" The Midnight Girls laughed against the neon window. "Come back, little darling. Come back."

CHAPTER TWENTY-TWO

Glory—5 Months Ago

Glory stood at the front door, sinking in the snow. She bit the insides of her cheeks to keep her teeth from chattering, almost drawing blood. The cold was worse than she'd remembered. Her hair was clumped and frozen. Snowflakes collecting on her eyelashes. Her nylons were soaked, toes numb in rigid heels. At least her feet didn't hurt anymore. She couldn't feel them.

This morning, at the Outer Island Motel, a little place in the woods behind town, she had spent an hour in the bathtub digging her nails into a bar of soap. She'd wanted to smoke so badly she'd had to dunk her pack underwater. She hadn't quit yet but wanted Marta to think that she had. After getting out of the tub, she'd slapped a nicotine patch onto her shoulder and sat on the floor, on a hideous dark stain, in front of a crummy mirror, agonizing over her hair, her makeup. Summertime foundation, too orange. She could feel it now, sliding across her face, wet with snow. She had chosen the yellow linen dress in the dim light of the motel room. But outside, she looked out of place, ridiculous. Her pink wool coat was ridiculous, too. Frilly and cheap, scratching at her neck. She hadn't bothered to try it on until stepping off the plane into sleeting Duluth.

She could feel the tiny white box in her pocket. Marta's gift. An orange blossom from Glory's backyard. An invitation to visit, small and unobtrusive. And if that weren't enough, if Marta needed something more substantial, there was always Glory's old homecoming dress, stashed under the bed. Bo was sentimental, a packrat. He'd probably left it there.

She should knock; of course she should. But what if he

answered? What would she say? "Hi, it's me. Remember?" Faking a laugh. "Please don't be angry, darling."

Would he kiss her? Cry? Get angry, after she'd asked him not to?

Would it be worse if Marta were the one to answer the door? She might take one look at her mother and say, "Who the heck are you?" or simply ignore her, like she would an Avon lady.

After seven years alone with her father, Marta would probably be furious. Those final moments stuck in her mind on a loop: her mother ironing all the dresses she had ordered from Penney's. Curling her hair into perfect waves, coughing through hairspray. Packing the curling iron, still hot, into an overstuffed suitcase. Complaining about the weight of it on the walk down the stairs. The clank of high heels. Slipping through the door. A smile—brief, without eye contact—at Marta pouting on the couch, toes tucked between the cushions. Her white nightgown speckled red from picked mosquito bites. "Be good, min kära." Her mother. Disappearing at the end of the driveway. Not turning back to wave.

Glory had been too distracted. As she'd trotted away from the house, she was imagining herself crossing the state line into sunny Florida and shedding the loneliness—and all that was wrong with her life—as quickly and easily as peeling off a winter coat. She felt ill now thinking of how giddy she'd been, how wrong, how oblivious to her daughter's loneliness, which must be powerful now.

But it wasn't too late. Glory could grab her suitcase, drag it back across the ice road into town. Keep dragging until she was far away. In Duluth. On an airplane. Home, in her sunny trailer, where she could hide for another seven years.

Oh, God.

She heard footsteps.

"Hello?" A defiant little voice, right behind her. "You need something?"

Glory froze.

Then Glory was lying on the bed pretending to sleep, Marta curled up beside her, so still and so perfect. Their meeting had been awful at first. Glory had come off as flippant, unapologetic, even—she blamed her nerves. She could feel Marta's anger, years of disappointment, disgust.

Thank God for the homecoming dress.

Marta had finally softened, just a little, enough to lie beside her, to let Glory hold her hand. Glory hadn't deserved that kindness, but someday, she might. Marta would come for a visit, and Glory would show her absolutely everything. They'd rent bicycles, feed seagulls from the boardwalk, play bocce ball, and visit some of her favorite patients at the nursing home where she worked. She would introduce Marta to the neighbor girl with the fuzzy dog. Send her home with a suitcase full of souvenirs. They'd write letters back and forth.

It was strange, this feeling of hopefulness, nearing joy. She could've held onto it a little longer, had she not been reminded of Bo.

The smell of him on the sheets, grassy, faintly sweet like damp firewood, made her heart ache. And when she'd finally seen him standing over the bed, she'd almost lost control. She'd wanted to kiss him. She'd wanted to feel the weight of his body pressing down on her, the comfort of being consumed in his bear hug. To hear the words "where do you think you're going?" whispered into her ear the moment she tried to tear away. But they weren't those people anymore. They would never possess that closeness. Even before leaving, she had severed the bond.

And now, she was back, and he was staring down at her, his eyes big and fragile, like he'd just seen a ghost. "You're back." It should've been a question.

She smiled—what else could she do?—and he moved toward her, almost tenderly.

"For a visit," she said.

And then he stopped. His whole body changed, rage creeping over him.

Glory sat up quickly. "Please don't be angry—"

"Outside." He grabbed her arm and dragged her off the bed.

He borrowed the neighbor's truck and drove her across the ice. "I don't want Marty to hear," he said. "I don't want her listening." An odd thing to say, she thought, because there was nothing to listen to. They weren't arguing. They barely spoke as the truck bounced over divots in the ice, tires croaking in the snow. He stared at the blackness ahead of them, as if deciding something. *What to do? What to do with her?* His fingers curled around the steering wheel, tighter and tighter, the pale skin of his knuckles stretched so thin she could see the veins in his hand. She shouldn't have told him where she was staying. She should've called Sylvia. She should've run as fast as she could—away.

He pulled into the parking lot at the Outer Island Motel and flipped off his headlights. "Which room?" he asked. When she didn't immediately answer, he said, "Give me the key." She dug around in her purse, stalling, the yellow plastic Room 5 keychain glaring up at her.

"It's not here," she said. "I can't find it. Let me ask the man at the front desk for help."

Before she had time to pop open the door, Bo grabbed her wrist and dragged her out the driver's side into the woods. It was so cold she could see her own screams hitting the air. Hundreds of yards away, up on the hill, was her old house, glowing, magnificent. In the second-story window, she could even glimpse the face of a woman. Was it Alice? Could she hear her? Why was she just standing there, watching them?

Glory struggled until her wrist snapped—distal radius fracture. Bo must've heard it, too, because he dropped her arm and, for a moment, she thought, *This is it. He's freaked himself out. He's letting me go.*

She was surprised at how good the snow felt on the back of her head, calming, as he pinned her to the ground. She should fight back—claw his face, bite whatever skin she could reach—but he was so much stronger, straddling her body. His knees digging into her wrists. His warm, calloused hands bruising her neck. She could feel his hatred. And, in those fragile eyes, his love for her, too, which had somehow survived all these years. Without it, he would've let her go. But it was clear now, on this cold winter night, her curls wilting in the snow, her face growing slack, that he wasn't going to let her get away again. Or get away with anything. It would be impossible now, far too late, to explain that she had suffered, too, more than he could imagine. And even if she had the time, the breath, an explanation wouldn't be enough. So she had suffered, so she was sorry. What he wanted was regret. But, given the same circumstances, even this outcome, she would've done it all again. Made the choices that led her to those perfect pastel trailers, to the nursing home, the other nurses, her patients, and a place that finally felt like home. His fingers were tighter now, her lungs aching. Instead of flailing or gasping or spitting in his eerie, tortured face, she concentrated on the snow beneath her, cool and quiet.

Here now, but not forever.

CHAPTER TWENTY-THREE

Marta

At the top of the hill, the chapel sat dark and still, glowing in the orange light. Starlings dove and swooped across the sky, rushing from the ghostly steeple in fantastic black swarms. This was the coldest hour of the day, near sunrise. My eyes stung. My body ached without sleep, but I'd kept running until I was here, at the base of the steeple, among the rotting nativity sets and mossy gravestones. The churchyard was overgrown with big bluestem so tall I couldn't read the names of the dead.

I shoved the chapel doors, but they were locked. The stained-glass windows along the sides of the building were boarded up. Some of them had been shattered by the kids at school. I could hear the snap of glass beneath my boots as I ran around back. There I found a window low enough to climb through. The glass had been knocked out, the lead frame punctured and twisted of out shape. My heart was beating so loudly I could no longer hear Sylvia calling for me at a distance. I pulled myself up, and toppled into the church, diving like the starlings.

There was pain first, at the crown of my head. I had smacked the wood floor with all the weight of my body. For a long time, I lay unmoving on the floor between pews. There was broken glass in my hair, blood on my hands.

And then I heard her calling from the altar. "I prayed for this. I knew you'd come."

High heels clicking.

Somewhere between awake and dreaming, I rubbed my eyes. My head ached. My ears were ringing. I couldn't stand. I tried to drag myself beneath a pew, but suddenly she was here. My mother—exactly as she'd looked seven years ago—too thin in a white floral dress, too pale, even blue at the wrists, but beautiful, terribly beautiful, after all this time apart. Her yellow hair was loose, toppling over her shoulders and hanging just above my face. Her lips were the color of Toast of New York. She was smiling. A small mischievous smile. "Do you believe in the Good Lord, min kära?"

She flung her head back and laughed, sending a delicate echo through the chapel. It was the sound Dad had wished to hear, the sound I knew by heart.

"Then it must be magic," she said. "Even in this town."

I reached out my hands and tried to sit up, but couldn't.

She frowned, pouting, and sat above me on the pew. She kicked her heels up on the kneeling bench. "Don't be cross with me. I've come a long way to get here. A long way for you."

"Can you help me up?"

She leaned forward. "The least you could do is say hello."

I touched her ankle. Her nylons were smooth and cold.

"Oh, my, you're bleeding. They'll stain." She scooted down the pew, tucking her legs beneath her, just out of reach. "This is the only pair I've got."

"What are you doing here?"

"You've missed me, haven't you? Say so, and I'll say how much I've missed you, too." She reached down and tucked my hair behind my ear. "I'll even fix you up."

"Dad made you come." I felt as though I had been hollowed out.

"Please, min kära. Say so."

"I missed you."

"A great deal?"

"A great deal."

She took both of my hands and lifted me up slowly, wavering in her high heels. She was taller than I was, so small around the waist that her ribs stuck out. It was strange how beautiful she was yet, at the same time, so unhealthy looking. Like that girl who'd skipped lunch for a semester and had been forced to leave our school. I clung to her—feeling how very fragile she was—as she lowered me onto the pew. She disappeared for a moment and came back again with her worn floral suitcase. She unzipped it, dug through a heap of dresses, and pulled out her tiny pink Avon bag. She plucked out one cigarette, tucked it under the sleeve of her dress, and went back to the Avon bag. She pulled out a tissue marked with kisses.

"There, there, my darling," she said, patting the tissue against the cuts on my palms. "Everything will be fine now."

The tissue puckered with blood. She pressed it down firmly. I winced.

She said, "See, it's not so hard to take care of you. I could've done it all along."

The window frame had scraped my skin, a shallow cut. I could feel a goose egg forming on the top of my head.

"Say how I could've done it," she said, wrapping her arm around me. She drew me tightly to her side and leaned her head against my shoulder. Her yellow hair was soft, sticky with hairspray. I wanted to pull away from her and run from the chapel, but I couldn't move. I didn't know what to say. I had spent so long wishing for her, searching for her, repeating in my mind all those things I had wanted to ask her. Now here she was. It was jarring how strange she felt. How unfamiliar.

"Say it. I need you to," she said.

"You could have."

"That's a good girl. Please don't listen to your father. He doesn't understand."

"He brought you here, didn't he? Sent you money for a ticket home?"

"Money?" She laughed, curls bobbing. "He doesn't have any."

"What about last winter, when you gave me that dress?"

"What about it?"

"Did he ask you to come then?"

"Of course not. I came back on my own. All that way just for you."

I wanted to believe her. She must've seen it in my sorry smile because she peered up at me and squeezed my scratched-up hand. "You have to believe me. Say you do."

Her hand was as cold as December. "I believe you," I said.

"I was about to come find you," she said. "But then I saw the chapel, this lovely old chapel. And when I came in—" She paused. "I didn't want to leave."

"Why not?"

She pressed her thumb to her lips. "I didn't want to see them. It didn't feel *right*."

"Them?"

"Sylvia. Your father." There was something dark in her expression. "Tell me how they are, how they look."

"They look fine."

"Does he love her?"

"He loves you."

She smiled for a second, then frowned. "Do you love her?"

I bit my lip. I didn't want to say it. I had never even allowed myself to think it. But, of course, I loved Sylvia. She was the only real mother I had.

"She's not anything." Her voice was flat, serious. "I'm your mother. You belong to me."

"You're my mother."

"That's a good girl."

Outside the chapel, the sun had risen. A sliver of light was pouring in through the broken window and it fell across her face like a spotlight. She leaned away from the light and kissed me on the cheek. "I have my own place, min kära, on a little canal. We have cranes in the morning, alligators in the afternoon, big and scaly, bathing in the sun. Orange blossoms year round."

I let her lean against me.

"You would love it," she said.

"I would love it."

"Maybe you'll come sometime."

"I'll come."

It was exactly what she wanted to hear. It should've made her happy. But when she looked at me, her smile fell and, with it, the warmth in her eyes, her whole expression. She looked like she had been punctured, a balloon sinking in the air. "You don't love me." No false ring in her voice. Nor was there anger. It was a statement. "You'll never forgive me."

"How can I?" It was the first honest thing I'd said to her.

"You aren't sorry."

She looked stunned. "Did you read the letters?"

"Yes."

"And?"

"They were empty, like you."

She was angry now. This was more comforting than those distant zombie eyes. "You don't know me. Did that ever occur to you?"

"Every day, actually. Back when you lived here, when you used to call, when you sent those letters. Poetic and dumb."

That made her laugh. "I was trying to be nice, to show you where I'd been."

"I don't care where you've been." My head was really hurting. "I wanted to know *you*."

She didn't understand how slippery she was—her personality, her state of being. Mother one moment, gone the next. Fake happy, crying in the bathroom. It was exhausting trying to understand who she was.

"I'm a nurse. Well, a CNA. Like an assistant," she said.

"Where do you work?"

"At a nursing home. The people are rude, worse than Grandpa Jan. But I've got friends there. Farah has a daughter your age. I was hoping you could meet her."

"In Florida?"

"On an island. It's a lot warmer than this. Summers are

terrible. If you're not in the pool, you have to stay inside. Move from one air-conditioned room to the next. Come to think of it, you'd probably hate it." She smiled.

"Didn't you miss me?"

"Are you kidding? Of course."

"What about Dad?"

Her lips made a line.

"Didn't you ever love him?"

"Oh, min kära, in the very beginning, I couldn't help myself." She drew the cigarette from her sleeve and lit up in the crook of her hand. "You have to remember how sweet he was. He didn't drink back then. It was simple pleasures—long drives at night, sneaking out my window onto the rooftop, laughing and splitting a cigarette and talking about a whole lot of nothing. He lived in the moment. Didn't want anything out of life, except for me. It was so nice forgetting how lonely I was." She paused. "Things change, and then again, they don't. At the end of the day, I was still that lonely kid. You know what that's like. It follows you."

I had spent so long feeling angry. Sure, I had wanted to find her, but I'd hated her too for what she'd done to us. I had never really thought of her as a person. Never considered what she had wanted out of life, only that it didn't involve being my mother.

For that, I had wanted her to suffer. I had wanted her to hate her life and come crawling back. To say, "You're enough for me." Though my father had never said as much, this is what he had wanted too. Why he had worked like crazy on the house. Remained single all these years, waiting for her to waltz back in.

And she had—on that cold December day, six months ago.

"What did he do to you?" I could feel my heart sinking. She was too thin. Too pale. Too beautiful. She hadn't aged. She looked the same as when she'd left seven years ago—not like the person who had come to our house, with her tan lines and crow's feet.

She took a drag. Long exhale. "Try to forgive him, won't you? Even though it's ugly. Even though it's wrong. He's got a temper, you know that." She flicked ash at the floor. "Maybe he thought I was going to take you away, I don't know."

Her expression was sweet and suffering, like Levi's at the lighthouse. We both knew this wasn't the reason. Dad wasn't worried about losing me. It was *her*. He wasn't going to lose her again. Not after all this time and all this wanting.

She pulled at the slender end of her cigarette until the sunlight was littered with haze. The smell made my stomach turn.

"I'm sorry," was all I managed to say. Sorry for hating you. For pinching my eyes shut when he got home, pretending to sleep because it was easier for me.

I grabbed her hand, trying to keep it warm. "I do love you. I always have."

She was my mother. I had loved her once and loved her still, when the lilacs bloomed, when Virginia Slims flooded the air. I loved her in photographs, in dreams. Only now, with my head aching and her eyes watering and all that phoniness gone, did I feel I actually knew her. Just a small part, something I could hold onto.

Maybe someday I would turn out like her. I would be the one to leave, and then I'd understand everything. Now I could only hear the small sounds of her crying, so quietly. And though I didn't understand why she needed to run so far or why it had taken so long for her to reach me, I wanted to make her smile again.

"I forgive you," I said. I knew she wouldn't ask twice. This was the only peace I could offer her.

She smiled, but she looked so tired, her face wet with tears.

"I have to leave," my mother said. "You understand, don't you?"

I nodded.

Though she was beside me, I could feel her presence drifting like the smoke. I held her hand until the cigarette burned down, and then I got up and left her there in the chapel. I knew my mother was gone. I knew no one would ever find her body. And I would spend forever wondering what had passed between my parents. An argument, a fight, more vicious than any time before, and then a crime, something Dad would call an accident. But, of course, it wasn't that simple. Even if he hadn't meant to kill her, he had wanted to hurt her—deeply, irreversibly, worse than she'd hurt him.

I could go to the police, tell them everything I knew or thought I knew. But what would happen then? They would take him away from me, and I would be left with even less.

And so I wouldn't say a word. Sylvia wouldn't either. We would hide the purse. Pretend it never happened. I would go back to school, Sylvia to the diner. And Dad would spend the rest of his days sulking, dulled by guilt, stricken by the love he had tried to make disappear.

I climbed back out the window, wove my way through the graveyard, and walked down the mainland hill. The town was bustling with early tourists flocking up and down the streets for their coffee and breakfast. I could see *the Island Queen* approaching from the island. The sun was inching above the horizon, throwing pink light across the lake.

I walked to the shore. Dipped my hand into the freezing water and felt for her there. Maybe my mother was beneath the surface, perfect and porcelain, drifting with the other bodies. Sleeping at the bottom of the lake.

A hundred million years ago, this place had belonged to a mountain range, then to glaciers as high as the Alps. The land had worn down slowly until there were soft rolling hills, twenty-two islands hollowed out by the waves, and the depths of a great lake. And then there were the Ojibwe, the French and the Jesuits, the mainland town, and the little gray chapel, which, like my mother, had come and gone. I wanted to kneel by the shore and watch it come back with force: the mountains sprouting up from the soil, the lake rising, spilling over, and the islands pulling back to shore, their hollows made whole in reverse. Every lost soul would rise up too. Emerging from the water like you would on a hot summer day after a long cold swim.

There was no greater feeling.

Acknowledgments

I want to start by thanking Sabina Murray, a writer I greatly admire, who chose this novel for the Juniper Prize. Thank you to everyone at the University of Massachusetts Press and the University of Massachusetts MFA program. Thank you to the University of California, Riverside, for supporting this project, and thank you to my writing teachers—Susan Straight, Jane Smiley, Charmaine Craig, Nalo Hopkinson, and Michael Jayme—for your conversation, your notes, and your work, which continues to inspire me. Thank you to Sterling HolyWhiteMountain and Lorrie Moore, two of my favorite writers and teachers from the University of Wisconsin, Madison. Thank you to my wonderful agent, Carrie Howland, and to the community of writers I was lucky enough to work with, especially Paula Tang, Lina Patton, Andy Holt, and Kate Wisel. Thank you to *Midwestern Gothic* for publishing the short story that would become the first chapter of this novel. Thank you to the Community of Writers in Olympic Valley, California, and thanks to Noah Ballard for his advice and feedback.

Many thanks to the Apostle Islands National Lakeshore community. I spent one summer living in Red Cliff and Bayfield but remained there in my mind for the next decade. Gichigami is the Ojibwe name for Lake Superior. I hope that my use of the word conveys the love and respect I have for this place and this community and my desire to honor it. The Juniper Prize monetary award will be donated to nonprofits that serve the Red Cliff community.

Thank you to the Madeline Island Museum for their historical and cultural resources, and to James Vukelich Kaagegaabaw for his great resources on the Ojibwe language.

Thank you to the friends I made up north—Alyssa Haukaas, Britt Sirrine, and the folks at the Old Rittenhouse Inn—and to the friends who read early drafts and kept me company on this long journey. And thanks to my in-laws for their support and enthusiasm.

Thank you to my family—my mother, Gail; my father, Joe; my sister, Natalie; and our cherished companions (Susie, Sunny, Tobi, Benny, Lady, Doug)—for your love, your lightheartedness, the long walks and summers spent out on the driveway.

Love and thanks to my husband, Joey. The best day of my life was spent with you and Susie on the island where this novel is set. I'll always remember your joy on those warm sandstone cliffs, the endless blue on the horizon.

LINDSEY STEFFES studied fiction at University of Wisconsin, Madison and has an MFA from University of California, Riverside, where she was mentored by Jane Smiley and Susan Straight. Her short story, "Gichigami," which later became the first chapter of this novel, was published in *Midwestern Gothic* Issue 17. Other work has been recognized by *Glimmer Train* and featured in *Atticus Review*, *Black Heart Magazine*, and *Sad Girl Diaries*. She was awarded the Dean's MFA Graduate Fellowship. She has taught creative writing as a fellow for the Gluck Fellows Program of the Arts. Lindsey lives in Minneapolis with her husband and two dogs.

JUNIPER
JUNIPER PRIZE FOR FICTION